The Runner and the Kelpie

Dave Duncan

Five Rivers Publishing
www.fiveriverspublishing.com

Pictish inscription, possibly a kelpie
image courtesy www.janetmcnaughton.ca

kelpie (noun) (Celtic folklore) A malevolent shapeshifting spirit, most often in the form of a horse, believed to haunt the rivers and lochs of Scotland.

Wiktionary

Published by Five Rivers Publishing, 704 Queen Street, P.O. Box 293, Neustadt, ON N0G 2M0, Canada

www.fiveriverspublishing.com

The Runner and the Kelpie, Copyright © 2014 by Dave Duncan

Edited by Dr. Robert Runté.

Cover Copyright © 2014 by Jeff Minkevics

Interior design and layout by Lorina Stephens

Titles set in Monotype Corsiva, designed by Patricia Saunders at the Monotype Corporation.

Byline and headers set in Trajan Pro, designed in 1989 by Carol Twombly for Adobe, based on Roman square capitals.

Text set in Century Schoolbook, originally designed by Linn Boyd Benton in 1894 for American Type Founders.

All rights reserved. Without limiting the rights under copyright reserved above, no part of this publication may be reproduced, stored in or introduced into a retrieval system, or transmitted in any form or by any means (electronic, mechanical, photocopying, recording or otherwise), without the prior written permission of both the copyright owner and the publisher of the book.

Publisher's note: This book is a work of fiction. Names, characters, places and incidents either are the products of the author's imagination or are used fictitiously, and any resemblance to actual persons living or dead, events, or locales is entirely coincidental.

Published in Canada

Library and Archives Canada Cataloguing in Publication

Duncan, Dave, 1933-, author

The runner and the kelpie / Dave Duncan.

Issued in print and electronic formats.

ISBN 978-1-927400-65-4 (pbk.).--ISBN 978-1-927400-66-1 (epub)

I. Title.

PS8557.U5373R843 2014   C813'.54   C2014-903363-X

C2014-903364-8

Contents

Chapter 1	5
Chapter 2	11
Chapter 3	23
Chapter 4	33
Chapter 5	41
Chapter 6	48
Chapter 7	54
Chapter 8	63
Chapter 9	68
Chapter 10	76
Chapter 11	85
Chapter 12	91
Chapter 13	96
About the Author	105
Books by Five Rivers	106

Chapter 1

When Ivor had been promoted to captain of the mormaor's runners, four months ago, he had been assigned a room of his own in the armoury building. That was a great honour for an unmarried man in the fort at Stiegle, especially one who hadn't even turned seventeen back then. But it meant that he wasn't sharing a shed with the other runners, so there was nobody to hear him scream.

He was screaming because he was sitting on marshy ground, with his wrists and ankles tied, and a monster was coming for him. He couldn't see it in the dark, except as a very pale shape, a sort of vague slightly-less-black in the blackness, but he could smell its horsey smell and hear its snuffling. Then it closed its teeth on his right leg. The pain was terrible, and he screamed even louder. It backed away, dragging him, but the rope around his wrists had been tied to the tree he had been leaning against, so his hands stayed where they were while the rest of him slid. His arms were twisted backward until they were wrenched out of their sockets, then his hands were crushed to paste when they were hauled through the rough rope bonds.

If he wasn't screaming his lungs out by then, he certainly ought to be. He said, *"Oh, St. Seumas, help me!"* and woke up.

He was lying on his pallet, soaked in sweat and gasping for breath. His blanket was all entangled around his legs, showing how he must have been struggling. He listened, but he couldn't hear anyone shouting, or beating on his door, so perhaps his screaming had only been part of the dream. But what a nightmare! He had never had one that bad before. He was very fit, running ten miles most days and sometimes a lot more than that, so he usually slept like a log—six and a half feet of pine.

It must mean something. Dreams that vivid always meant something. He had heard many stories of people dreaming of their own deaths, or loved ones' deaths, and then, two or three weeks later.... But what could he do about this one? Who could advise him?

Gruoch, that's who! Gruoch was the local wise woman, able to interpret dreams, read palms, foretell the sex of unborn babes, or explain whose curse had caused a sudden sickness. Gruoch, in short (and only in a whisper) was a Weird. He must go and ask Gruoch. Trouble was, only women went to visit her, in her hovel on the hillside. Men didn't, or if they did, they did so in secret, by night.

What time was it, anyway? Having no window, Ivor's private room might more honestly be called a cubicle, or even a closet by anyone wanting to start a fight. But he couldn't hear feet going by his door, so it must still be dark. The gates of Stiegle Fort were closed at sunset and opened at sunrise, and absolutely nobody could order them opened sooner—nobody except Mormaor Malcolm himself, or Uvan son of Domlech, his senior housecarl... or Ivor of Glenbroch, his captain of runners. If Ivor so much as told the night watch that one of his team might come home before dawn, that would be authority enough to admit him.

Ivor scrambled around in the dark to find his clothes: leggings, smock, shirt, and blanket, which served as his cloak by day. He wore shoes only when it had snowed or he was going riding. He quietly opened the door, and was happy to hear faint snores from other rooms. Then he remembered that anyone going to consult Gruoch had better take her a gift. He racked his brains for a moment before recalling that he had a spare candle somewhere that he'd never used. That would do, if he could find it.

It was still night, but dawn was close enough that the kitchen serfs were awake, stoking up the fires. He trotted around that way and collected a piping hot bannock to eat on the run. With butter dribbling down his chin, he came to the gate and found the guards nodding at the end of their watch. They grumbled at having to open the gate for him, because there was a drill they must follow, to ensure that no enemy was lurking outside, but they didn't ask him where he was going or why it couldn't wait. They knew he wouldn't tell them.

He set off down the hill at a slow lope, the gravelly surface cold under his feet. About halfway to the town, a faint path led off to his left, so faint that he almost missed it in the twilight. He would have to be quick, because if anyone at the fort learned that he'd been to see Gruoch, he would never hear the last of it. A seventeen-year-old man visiting a Weird would be suspected of having got some girl in trouble or—worse—of wanting to buy a love charm. Father Crinan would summon him and lecture him on the fate of his soul, for Jesus had not yet driven all the ancient gods out of Alba. Evil spirits still lurked in the remoter parts of its glens and moors.

From the outside, Gruoch's home looked like a pile of sticks and turf, more of an animal's lair than a house. Ivor surveyed it with dislike. A nearby spring explained how she could live here at all, but she must depend on the women of the town to keep her supplied with food. Some of them might be on their way to see her even now, so he would have to be quick, for the sky was growing brighter by the minute. A red dawn was an omen for bad weather ahead, especially with the harvest not all in yet.

"Gruoch!" he said loudly. "Anyone home? Gruoch?" After a moment, he repeated, "Anyone home?"

Came a croak: "Aye, she's home. What's a braw young lad like you doing visiting a Weird like old Gruoch?"

He couldn't see her, so how could she see him? Then he realized that even he could tell the timbre of a young man's voice from an older's.

"I brought you a present, Goodwife."

Cackle. "I'm no wife, good or no. Come in then and welcome."

Ivor sank to hands and knees and crawled in. The inside smelled even more like an animal's lair than the outside looked. Trying not to gag, he held out the candle, and it was removed from his grip.

"Aye, a rich gift indeed!" the old woman rasped, and she was no more visible than the monster in his dream. "So what do you want in return, young sir—you with a silver buckle on his belt and a silver ring on his thumb?" She must have the eyes of an owl!

"I had a dream...."

"A dream, is it? And what young man doesn't dream of the girl he fancies?"

"No, not like that!" There was a girl he fancied a lot, but he didn't *dare* dream about her—Malcolm would kill him. "A monster."

The old woman made a sound that might have indicated surprise. "Give me your hand then, lad. No, the left one." Two bundles of fingers like knobbly dry sticks closed around his hand. One of them wandered up his forearm and then went back to join with the other. "You're younger than I thought, but older than you seem." Long pause. "You bear heavy burdens that mortals cannot see."

She was hinting at the messages he carried, but he was not impressed with her magic, because he could guess that she had recognized his runners' belt buckle.

"Tell me then," she wheezed. "Tell me of this dream that so wracks a young man's soul."

He told her what he could remember. Already the details were starting to blur. Why had he been so scared, like a baby? He had wasted a perfectly good candle and risked making a public fool of himself.

For a long time the old crone said nothing, but the grip of her gnarled hands did not slacken, so he could not just leave, which is what he very much wanted to do now. The sun would be up.

"You will go on a sad, sad journey."

Of course he would go on a journey! That was his job—running over half Alba carrying messages from Malcolm—and he did it very well.

"You will try to save a fair maiden."

That sounded more like a job for a swordsman than a boy with strong lungs and a good memory, but she hadn't said he would succeed. For every famous hero rescuing damsels there must be a dozen meatheads who just screwed up. He was going to protest or perhaps even laugh, but the grip on his hand tightened in warning. So there was more to come, but it took times, while the Weird moaned as if in distress. Then she groaned.

"You will meet the monster and when help comes, you will refuse it."

She released him. "Go!" she cried. "The sun is up... go... go now!"

"Oh, well, thank you." He backed out into the so-welcome fresh air. There was nobody in sight, and the edge of the sun had just topped the hills. It was over, thank the saints. How stupid he had been! Meet a monster and refuse help? What nonsense! Rain was starting to fall, so the weather had broken. He ran back to the fort for breakfast and the day guards welcomed him home as if he had been away for days.

Chapter 2

One morning a couple of weeks later, when Ivor had managed to forget about his stupid dream and even stupider visit to the Weird, he dived into the runners' shed, slammed the door behind him, threw back his hood, and flapped his cloak to shake water off the oily wool. The only person present was Ilgarach, the oldest runner, who had been lying on a lower bunk, staring at the boards above him. He stood up and greeted his chief with a leer of jagged broken teeth, the result of slipping while fording a stream and landing face-first on a rock. He was quite proud of the effect, because it made him look like a fighter.

He said, "God bless, Cap'n."

"And bless you, too. Anyone else back yet?"

Ilgarach nodded. "Edan got in late last night. He's still stuffing his gut in the hall."

When the weather had broken, the mormaor had begun sending the boys out to learn the state of the harvest in his earldom. But nobody travelled fast on mud. Half the fords would be impassable already. Galan and Gest, the other two runners, might be gone for days more.

"The earl wants me to report to him an hour after sunrise," Ivor said.

"And how does he expect you to know when that is, under a sky like a layer of peat?"

"If you've finished breakfast and Edan hasn't, that would be about right, I'd say."

The ogre grin again... "And when he has finished, that would be two hours after?"

"Likely! I don't have a clue what Malcolm has in store for just us. Stick around where I can find you."

Ilgarach just shrugged. "Not much else to do. You know something, Cap'n? We have it better than the housecarls in winter. At least we do get out sometimes. All they have to do is pick fights."

Ivor laughed. "But that's all they're good at!" He flipped his hood over his head and sprinted off into the downpour again. Every river and stream was going to be in spate, and then even the runners wouldn't be going anywhere. Winter was always boring. Today was especially bad, water coming down in barrelfuls, so everyone was running. Even fat old cooks were splattering along through the mud as fast as they could move. Summer had ended; winter could not be far behind.

From the shed to the mormaor's personal quarters was a brief run. The two guards on the door had a porch to shelter them, but looked chilled. They saluted Ivor, a sign of respect that they would not normally extend to any mere runner, even the chief one. So far as he knew, Malcolm had not ordered that, but all the men in the fort had been doing it ever since Ivor had been credited with working a miracle, back in the summer.

"He said he'd be back soon, and to let you in, Captain."

Ivor thanked them and went in. The reception room was the second largest in the fort, after the great hall. It was dim, lit by faint winter light filtered through parchment windows, and by a glowing peat fire on the hearth. Again shaking his cloak—the cloak his mother had woven for him long ago, before she died—he headed for that fire like a moth to a candle. Then he hesitated, seeing that Lady Meg was already there.

Meg was three months younger than he, head and shoulders shorter, and breathtakingly, stunningly beautiful. Alas, she was Malcolm's daughter, and in public he would bow low to her, address her as, "My lady," but never speak to her unless she spoke to him first—which she would never have reason to do, for he was only a boy runner, not even a sword-wielding housecarl. But a careful look around told him that they was no one else present, so he strode eagerly over to her.

She was already raising her face. He wrapped her firmly in his arms, stooped, and kissed her. This was only the third time they had kissed, and it was insane. It was crazy. If they were discovered, he would be lucky to escape with a thorough whipping and a one-way dispatch back to Glenbroch in disgrace. But, oh, it was worth it!

Sometimes when he ran on the moor for exercise, he would meet her out riding, and then they might go a few miles together, with her official escort riding a tactful distance behind, but those were almost their only chances for conversation.

It was Meg who broke off the kiss, but she did not release him, just pressed her face against his chest. He held her there, feeling his hand cold against her flushed cheek. He was unsteady on his feet. *Madness, madness, madness!* As a child he had watched all his nine older brothers fall into this insanity of love, one after the other, and now it was his turn. But why did his obsession have to fall on the one woman he could never have?

Meg turned away to look at the fire. "That was very rash of you, Chief Runner."

"I know. I'm sorry."

She spun around angrily. "*Sorry?*"

"Sorry to have put you in danger, I mean. But that was the best moment of my life so far."

She looked down at the floor and whispered, "Mine, too."

"Oh, Meg, dearest Meg, what are we to do?"

"We are to wait here until my father returns. Then I will be put on display again, and you will be sent off to Glen Dorcha to discuss my dowry." Now her redness was a flush of anger, not passion.

Glen where? Ivor stared at her in horror. Only now he saw that she was wearing richer clothes than usual. Her gown was a shimmering pale blue that matched her eyes, and she wore a silver necklace above a lower than normal neckline. Her arms were bare except for four or five gold bracelets, so it was no surprise she was staying close to the fire. Her long hair, so blond as to be almost flaxen, hung loose to show that she was unmarried. Her eyes were red, and not all the damp seeping through his shirt was rain; some of it was tears.

Marriage had always been inevitable. Her father was a powerful man, the king's great steward for the western third of the kingdom. He would not marry his daughter off to any humble housecarl, let alone an insignificant boy runner. She would marry an earl, or a prince, for political advantage. It was rumoured that the king of Dublin had asked for her hand two years ago, but that Malcolm's overlord, King Constantine, had forbidden the match.

Meg moved closer to the fire, where she wrung her hands and stared into the glowing depths. "Oh, Ivor, I am frightened!"

He followed. Standing close behind her, he clasped her

shoulders. "I expect all women are frightened before they get married, but most of them seem happy enough afterward."

"But I want to marry a man, not just a name, or a title. Someone I can see when I close my eyes! I'm going to be contracted to a person I perhaps won't even meet until our wedding day. I will have to swear to love and obey him, to serve him all my life, bear his children.... I won't know if he's a hunchback or a drooling, cretinous, monster."

Ivor could think of nothing better to say than, "I'll warn you if he is." The fact that he had been summoned here meant that he was to be involved in this horrible matter somehow. Glen where had she said? Glen Dork? Maybe Malcolm would let him send one of the others.

"That will be very kind of you!" she snapped. "But not very helpful."

"Your father won't give you to some monster. He did let you choose Tasgall, didn't he?" Meg had been betrothed to Thane Tasgall of Glenbroch until he was slain at the battle of Nilcaster in the summer. Ivor had never dared ask her whether she had been in love with him, or just obedient to her parents' wishes.

"Father chose Tasgall, I didn't. He did ask me if I objected," she admitted. "I consented because I knew what Tasgall looked like! He was an impressive man, and I had spoken with him, and his obvious, um, desire for me was flattering. And," she added after a moment, "Glenbroch is not far away. I could hope I would be able to visit here sometimes, have Mother visit and.... Oh, Ivor, I think I'm going to start weeping again."

"Nonsense! You—" Hearing the outer door creak, he hastily moved away from her and turned to see who had come.

Earl Malcolm of Stiegle was large, imposing, and as fair in colouring as his daughter. At the moment, he was

THE RUNNER AND THE KELPIE

wearing workaday, almost shabby, jerkin and britches, stark contrast to her finery. That would be a deliberate choice, but Ivor did not know what message it was sending, or to whom.

The most likely recipient was the stocky young man who followed the mormaor in. "Stocky" was a compliment, for he was at least a head shorter than Ivor; indeed, he could not be much taller than Meg, so they would be well matched there. He wore a black beard cut square, he was as wide as a barrel, and he reminded Ivor of someone or something. His arrogant swagger suggested that he was a swordsman, although he was presently unarmed, because no visitor ever brought a sword into his host's private dwelling. Or his roll might just be caused by too wide a torso on too narrow a base.

While the guards closed the door, the newcomers headed for the fire, wiping water off their hands and faces—not quite like wet dogs shaking themselves, but not completely unlike, either. Ivor thought he saw Malcolm glance from him to Meg and back, as if wondering what they had been talking about. Had he seen Ivor jump away from her? *Saints, preserve me, his cloak had left damp marks on her gown!*

Girl and boy moved even farther apart, so the men could draw in, close to the hearth. The stranger bowed to Meg, who acknowledged him with a nod, so he could not be a thane, just a commoner. She would not be going to marry a commoner, but obviously they had met before, likely last night. And, since her complaint had been about having to marry a man she had never met, this could not be the suitor.

Malcolm took notice of Ivor, who bowed. "This is my captain of runners, Ivor of Glenbroch. Ivor, meet Drosten of Cleish, housecarl to Thane Elpin of Glen Dorcha."

Ivor bowed again—not quite as low as he had bowed to the mormaor, but respectful enough for a boy being presented to a swordsman. Inevitably the man looked surprised to hear that someone so young had been promoted to chief of anything more important than dung shovelling.

"I think I saw some brightening in the west," the earl told the housecarl. "With God's blessing, the rain will stop when the tide turns."

"I hope so, my lord, or my horse will have to swim all the way home."

"It will take a while for the rivers to fall," Malcolm agreed. "Of course you are welcome to stay until the journey seems safe. Ivor is my trusted confidant. When you leave, he will accompany you to deliver my reply to the thane."

That was strange. If this Drosten had brought the question, why couldn't he take back the answer? Thane and earl could not exchange letters, for only priests and monks were literate. Malcolm would have to dictate his reply to Father Crinan or Bishop Pol, who would write it down in Latin, and Elpin would have to have a priest read it to him, translating it into Pictish or Gaelic, whichever he spoke.

Drosten looked at Ivor's legs. "I hope you have a horse tall enough for him, my lord."

Ivor had noted for years that people shorter than he liked to make jokes about his height, and now that was practically everybody. He smiled politely: *Chew it well and swallow, Shorty.*

"Not many," Malcolm said. "Meg, you have some questions to put to Swordsman Drosten. About Dorcha, or Thane Elpin?"

Meg didn't hesitate, so the exchange had been planned. "I was thrilled to hear what a ferocious warrior my future husband is, and the extent of his lands and herds, but you didn't mention how old the thane is."

"He is of an age with myself, my lady, twenty-three."

"Is that not old for a man to be entering into matrimony?"

The man blinked at that fast response, but Ivor noticed his hesitation, so it was certain that the others did so too. "His lordship has been married before, my lady. His wife, lady Lilias, died most tragically... about a year ago."

"How?"

"She drowned. It was a very stormy night, and the thunder made it hard to sleep—it always echoes among the hills. She was a light sleeper, and the thane thinks she might have heard the horses spooked by the noise and gone out to calm them, then lost her way. Her cloak was found floating in the loch."

Meg gasped. "How horrible!"

"It was indeed, my lady. The whole glen mourned."

"Did she leave children?"

Housecarls were not accustomed to being interrogated by damsels, and this time the pause was more obvious. "Two daughters."

"Oh, the poor darlings! How old are they?'

"About four and... I'm not sure. A babe in arms yet, my lady."

"You didn't mention this last night," Malcolm said coldly.

"The thane did not consider it relevant, my lord, unless perhaps his ability to sire children was ever questioned. Of course he told me to tell you the sad story if you asked, as your daughter just did. And he mentioned that he would be willing to foster his daughters out, if her ladyship so requested."

So the omission had been deliberate. Despite the fire, the atmosphere had turned icy. Malcolm glanced at the parchment-covered windows. "I do believe it's getting brighter out there. Perhaps you will be able to start your journey home tomorrow, housecarl. As I said, Ivor will go with you."

That was dismissal. Looking unhappy, the emissary bowed to Meg and her father, ignored Ivor, and headed for the door. Not having been given leave, Ivor remained.

Hope burned in Meg's eyes brighter than the fire.

Her father shook his head. "There is no blame on a man for needing a second wife. Or on a widow for marrying again. I could name you men in Stiegle who have been married three times or more. I am a little disturbed that Drosten didn't mention the first marriage and the children right away, but that may be his fault, not Elpin's. Remember that a swordsman is not a trained message bearer like Ivor. Just one year's mourning is not overlong, I agree, but the man must be eager to make sons to follow in his footsteps."

He hadn't come right out and said that he wasn't going to change his mind, but that was obvious. Meg nodded, curtseyed to him, and walked stiff-backed over to the inner door, through which she disappeared into the family's private quarters.

Malcolm dropped into a padded chair and said, "Sit down."

In the half year that Ivor had been working for him, he had never told Ivor to sit in his presence. Even when Ivor had been running messages to and from the king for eight consecutive days, he had been left standing to deliver his final report. But he obeyed, and was astonished to discover how comfortable the big cushioned chair was.

For a long minute the mormaor stared into the worms of fire crawling over the peats on the hearth. "It's complicated," he said at last. "Elpin is a wealthy man, with broad lands, and a great many housecarls and crofters. He led one of the largest, if not the largest, hird in the king's army this summer. I know very little about him as a person, though. See if you can find out how his housecarls feel about him— that's always the best way to judge a thane, but of course you'll have to be very tactful in how you go about it.

"As part of his marriage proposal, he offers me Uachdar

Moor, which divides my thanedom of Ardenfort into two, and would be a good fit. He claims it's fine cattle grazing, with some peat digging and deer hunting. Go around by there if you can and see if he's telling the truth. Furthermore, we must still discuss Meg's dowry, so he may be dropping hints that I should give him Ardenfort itself. Either way, the marriage will involve large transfers of lands and changes of allegiance that could alter the balance of power in the west. The king will have to approve whatever we decide. He may well choke on the idea, and forbid the match."

Ivor squirmed uneasily. Normally the mormaor just dictated the message he wanted delivered, including the name of the person to whom it was addressed, and that was that. Ivor might send one of the others, or take the job himself, in which case he would visit the kitchen to load his satchel up with rations, and then head for the gate, or the stable on the rare occasions when he needed a horse. He might be gone a few hours or several days. Nowadays his memory was so trusted that he was never asked to speak back even the longest message. But when Malcolm began explaining things to him, it meant that the situation might become complicated, and he was going to be told to do more than just act as a mobile echo.

"My message to Elpin will be a simple agreement to the marriage and an invitation to come here and negotiate terms, *subject to the king's approval.* So when you have delivered my words to Glen Dorcha, I want you to go on to Scone and inform the king. You can tell Elpin what you plan, and he may send Drosten with you, or he might ask you to return here by way of Dorcha to tell him what Constantine said. Still with me?"

"Yes, my lord."

"Marriage contracts are never announced until they have been signed and sealed, because if the negotiations fail, one party or even both may be left feeling insulted. Feuds have started over less. The only people who know about this, here in Stiegle, are me, my wife and daughter, and now you; and in Glen Dorcha, probably only Elpin himself and Drosten, who must be one his most trusted housecarls. This is all very secret!"

"Of course, my lord!" Ivor did not manage to keep all his irritation out of his voice. Malcolm knew perfectly well that all his runners were sworn to secrecy. Ivor did not even let them discuss their errands among themselves.

If Malcolm noticed the sharp tone, he did not comment. "You cannot possibly leave until tomorrow, perhaps later. Do you want to wait until then to hear the messages?"

"As your lordship pleases. I won't forget them."

"The one to the king first, then...."

Ivor got up.

The earl smiled. "Would you rather I stood, also?"

"Er, I think so, my lord. It is how I was trained."

"Fair enough." He rose. "Hear my words. Give His Grace his full titles, but this is a personal matter, so just style me Earl Malcolm of Stiegle, saying: *I most humbly beg Your Grace's permission to discuss terms of a possible joining in matrimony of your noble Thane Elpin of Glen Dorcha and my daughter, including the extent of her dowry. Thus spake....* You notice that I left out any mention of allegiance? That matter can be raised later."

Ivor saw snakes in the grass already. "And if His Grace asks me whether it has been discussed, my lord?"

Malcolm frowned. "I don't see why— You know perfectly well that you are only a runner, to receive and deliver messages. You don't answer questions or comment on my business."

Easy enough for him to say that, but he wouldn't be the one facing an angry monarch. "Of course, my lord."

Malcolm scowled. "God's nails! He knows how much I

trust you, and he will ask. If you refuse to say, he'll eat you alive. Tell him the truth as you know it."

Nasty! That vague instruction was even worse, and could land Ivor in serious trouble.

"You may advise Elpin of my message to His Grace, and he may wish to be associated with it. If so, change the wording accordingly."

Again easy to say, but not easy to do.

"And now," Malcolm continued, "my answer to Elpin. Hear my words. My full titles... *greets noble Thane Elpin of Glen Dorcha, saying: your offer for the hand of Meg, my daughter, is pleasing to my ears. My runner will proceed to Scone to advise His Grace of our intent, and seek his blessing on our negotiations. With His Grace's approval secured, you shall be most welcome to make all haste to Stiegle that we may embrace you and smooth the path to the happiness you seek.* Any questions?"

"None, my lord." Except maybe, *Where should I puke?*

The mormaor nodded. "Drosten will advise you when he thinks the road should be passable."

Ivor bowed and departed. The girl he loved was going to be traded away for a few cows, and he had to help Malcolm close the sale. Horror of horrors! He walked to the door kicking his heart along the floor in front of him, because it was too heavy to carry.

Chapter 3

It was two days before Drosten declared himself ready to attempt the journey. Ivor had used the respite to run down to the town—which had no more buildings than the fort did but included some traders' stalls—and buy himself a leather cloak for rainy weather. It was probably older than he was, but he had never been able to afford such a luxury before he was appointed chief runner.

He tried not to mope, but he kept recalling the Weird's prophecy: *"You will go on a sad, sad journey."* It was true that he had never had to deliver a message he disliked as much as this one, but he had no choice. He had sworn an oath to report Malcolm's words correctly. He had a duty to do, and a family reputation for loyal service to live up to.

For a horse, he picked out Gawkie, a six-year-old bay gelding who had no great turn of speed but would plod along steadily for hours. He was reliable, sure-footed, and imperturbable; he was also tall like an overgrown colt, and therefore an all-around suitable match for his rider. Drosten rode a showy grey stallion that thought he knew better than his rider, and gave him much trouble for the first hour. Gawkie watched their antics patiently, once in a while flicking his ears with what Ivor suspected was disgust, but might have been envy.

Drosten himself had an irritating habit of whistling tiny fragments of melody, over and over. He stopped doing so only when he wanted to ask questions, which was almost as bad. Obviously he been asking about Ivor, and wanted to hear all about the miracle at Dunfaol. Ivor explained, as he always did, that he had done nothing except follow the instructions he had been given by ancient Saint Seumas. That holy man was the one who deserved the credit; recently word had come that he had died, but that had not been unexpected.

Ivor had decided what Drosten reminded him of: one of the great standing stones that dotted the moors, square-cut and solid. He was probably about as smart, too. That made him an odd choice to be a thane's most trusted housecarl, but they were the same age, so he had probably been a boyhood buddy. Intelligence was not essential for a swordsman in a battle; in fact it could be a deterrent, as Ivor's brother Jock had told him several times. What was needed was strength, stamina, and bloody-minded determination to stand fast and slaughter the enemy. Drosten might qualify on all counts.

Although the rain had stopped, the sky was low and gray, and the wind blustery. At first Ivor chose the route, since he knew the country. They crossed the Moor of Edan, which had once been dangerous territory for anyone from Glenbroch, but was now quite safe for Ivor, because he wore the silver belt buckle of the mormaor's runners and a ring with the king's wild boar emblem. With those, he would not likely be molested anywhere in Alba. Soon after that, though, Drosten veered off to the north, into lands Ivor did not know.

The country grew more mountainous and the wind colder. They paused a while to let the horses drink and graze. Soon after they resumed their journey they came to an angry river they dared not try to ford.

"Four days ago yon was but a wee burn," Drosten grumbled. He had ridden from Glen Dorcha to Stiegle in a single day, but his return looked likely to take longer.

Conversation was spotty, because both men wanted to find out more about the other's lord, and neither was willing to gossip.

"Twenty-three is young to be a thane," Ivor remarked at one point.

"Aye. But Glen Dorcha's been ruled by the same two families since Noah cut planks for the ark—turn and turn about, you understand. The Sons of Irb and the Sons of Uven, they're called."

"Elpin's father was tanist, a Son of Uven, and highly respected. When he died, couple of years ago, Elpin was elected to replace him, out of sympathy, mostly. Thane Breth was still hale and strong, and no one expected him to die so soon. But when he was called to glory, there was Thane Elpin. Nothing strange about it," Drosten concluded, with a challenging look.

A tanist was a thane's heir, elected by the swordsmen of the hird. The tanist could be either the thane's loyal deputy or his deadly rival, constantly plotting to succeed.

Nothing strange except that Elpin had apparently lost his father and his lord and his wife, in fairly quick succession. Such a rash of deaths suggested a curse. Ever since Ivor had met Rorie of Ytter, he had firmly believed in curses, just as Saint Seumas had convinced him of the power of blessings.

"And when was that—Breth's death, I mean?"

"Don't remember exactly," Drosten said, as if realizing he might have revealed too much. He was Elpin's confidant, after all, the most trusted of his housecarls. The thane wouldn't want Malcolm's emissary going home with a head full of gossipy rumours, much as Ivor might like to.

They came to a fertile valley, where the harvest had been successfully gathered before the bad weather set in, and there they stopped to feed the horses their oats and eat their own smoked fish and bannocks. Drosten couldn't whistle and chew at the same time, which was a blessing. He could talk that way, though.

"Why're you called a runner instead of just a messenger?" he asked.

"Because mostly I run. In winter I need more baggage and a horse to carry it. A horse is always faster over short trips, of an hour or so. But for anything farther and in good weather, I go faster on foot."

Drosten made sceptical noises, so Ivor explained how horses had to stop and graze for hours, while he could eat on the move if he had to. He bragged that he could run down anything on four legs as long as he could keep it in sight; then conceded that he wasn't sure about wolves—they might do the running down.

Drosten certainly wasn't lacking in courage, although his brains might be called into question, because after the meal, he proposed to ford the river, which was foaming along in spate. Ivor thought he was crazy to take such a risk—it wouldn't bring on the Last Trump if Meg had to stay unmarried one more day—and Gawkie agreed with him, balking at the water's edge. Drosten and his big stallion, having made it safely to the far side, turned and look back.

Ivor called, "You ride on, sir. We'll follow." Gawkie watched them go and whinnied at being left behind. "Up to you, coward!" Ivor sent a quick prayer to St. Seumas and dug in his heels. Reluctantly Gawkie went down the bank and eased his way across, one hoof at a time.

After that, they forded two more horrible rivers, and then

trekked up a long slope into the clouds. Drosten certainly seemed to know where he was going. This was, he explained, Uachdar Moor, which Thane Elpin was offering in trade for Meg. He didn't put it those words, though.

"You mean we've been in Malcolm's territory until now, all this way?"

No, Drosten explained. The boundaries were all zigzag. They'd crossed some other thanes' territories, but Ardenfort lands lay over *that* way—he pointed into the fog—and adjoined this moor, and the thane of Ardenfort was Malcolm himself. Malcolm had wanted Ivor's opinion of the moor, but that wasn't going to be much use if he couldn't see it. All he could tell was that it was mostly flat or gently rolling, with a lot of lonely rocks and big stones on the higher parts and boggy ground in the hollows. Within his limited field of view he saw no deer droppings or peat cuttings. And how was he ever going to find his way home again?

He asked Drosten how he knew which way to go.

"By the wind," the housecarl said smugly. "There is a breeze, if you watch the way the fog's moving. On terrain like this it's fairly constant, so I'm keeping it just forward of my left shoulder. And there are markers. Look there." He pointed to a line of three rocks close together.

Shortly after that the wind must have changed slightly, because he couldn't find the next marker and had to backtrack. He did find the way again, but he had definitely been worried for a while, which made Ivor feel both better and worse.

"Something's been grazing here," Ivor said.

"Either deer or cattle. The kine are mostly feral, though, and hard to catch. If you were coming this way on your own little feet, sonny, and met one of the wild bulls, you'd end up flatter than a cowpie."

Ivor had experienced some close calls with bulls. "Makes

the job interesting," he said. He also knew deer scats from cattle dung. Eventually he did see both, also some horse droppings, but those might have been left by travellers' mounts.

A sudden descent brought them below the clouds again, angling down into a steep-sided glen. This, Drosten proclaimed, was Glen Dorcha. When they reached the bottomlands, he suggested they dismount and let the horses eat again.

"How much farther?"

"Depends." Drosten eyed the clouds. "If we get to the loch while there's still daylight, it's only another hour. If we don't, then we overnight. There's a shelter there, of sorts. There are paths along both sides of the loch, but they aren't safe at night."

Ivor did not ask why they were unsafe. He dismounted as Dorsten did, and began removing the horses' bits and bridles so they could eat. He was tired and saddle-sore. In decent weather, he would have made much better time from Stiegle to here on foot.

▶▼◀

An hour or so after they resumed their travels, they came to a small river—the Dorcha, of course. Drosten pulled a face at the swirling brown water. "Can't ford that," he said, to Ivor's relief. "So we'll have to take the low road." He led the way upstream, soon arriving at the source, where it drained out of a small lake—Loch Dorcha, of course, and good trout fishing, according to Dorsten.

He pointed out the shelter he had mentioned earlier, a remarkably unattractive hovel of dry stone walls and a roof of turfs, about quarter of a mile away, uphill. There might be room for two men to crawl inside it, but it looked more like a dog kennel than a home for honest Christians. And why put it so far from the trail and the river?

Drosten studied the clouds doubtfully. "Yon's the high

road," he said, pointing to the far side of the river. "It goes up and down a fair bit; definitely no' safe at night."

Ivor could see that the far side was steep enough to be mostly bare rock, with little greenery at all. Since fording the Dorcha had already been ruled out, that left what must be known as the low road. The near side of the loch was straighter, not quite as steep, and surprisingly thickly forested.

"I think we can make it before dark," Dorsten said doubtfully. "You happy to go on? Two of us should be safe enough." Was there any real danger, or was he just having fun with the stranger?

"You're the guide, sir. You dare, I'll dare."

The housecarl nodded and kicked his mount, which was so weary that its usual effort to bite him was barely half-hearted. Riding through a forest was a rare experience for Ivor, and he never did enjoy it. At least this track was fairly level, well marked, and well used, as shown by the amount of animal droppings on the ground—horse, and deer—and also by their tracks, but it was so narrow that the travellers had to ride in single file. The footing was made treacherous by roots, mossy stones, and small boggy patches. Trailing branches threatened to poke out eyes, and were hard to see under the cloud-sodden sky. The air was full of unusual scents. On the brighter side, the trickier going did stop Dorsten's whistling.

Once or twice, where the dying light broke through the trees, Ivor thought he saw spoor he did not recognize, like an unshod horse's but much larger. He was far too weary to bother stopping to look. He had much rather think of trout. He had tasted trout only twice before in his life.

On his left, the forest sloped steeply upward. On his right it, varied from a few yards wide to nothing at all, when the horses had to splash their big feet through the shallow edges of the lake. Sometimes the bottom was sandy, sometimes pebbly or even rocky, but this would clearly be a dangerous route in the dark. Ivor had led a horse through worse, though, and wondered why Dorsten had made such a fuss about it.

The forest ended at last, revealing the walls of the glen and the end of the loch not far ahead. There were buildings in sight beyond it, which must be Dorcha itself. Darkness was definitely closing in, but the swordsman began his aimless whistling again, so all must be well.

Soon Ivor could make out that there was no fort in Dorcha, just a large hall and a spread of tiny cottages around it. If Thane Elpin ruled such a large and rich domain as Malcolm thought, it was strange that he chose to live in a bleak spot like that glen. On the other hand, the bottomlands there were clearly good farmland and the site was defensible. It would be hard to bring an army along the forest track, and on the other side of the loch—the high road—invaders would be very visible as they trekked up and down over the bare rock.

Two housecarls came galloping out to meet the newcomers, and hailed Drosten with respect, suggesting that he was either a highly esteemed fighter or just a close friend of the thane. He introduced Ivor as a guest, without giving his home or duties. They nodded a welcome to him, but judged him too young and unarmed to justify a salute.

Then the elder of the two said, "And how was the weather in Scone, Runner?" He had noticed the ring. The younger looked puzzled, and so did Drosten, which confirmed Ivor's suspicions that he had the brawn of an ox and the brains of a dormouse.

Ivor said, "Even the king must get rained on, sir."

The housecarl nodded, amused that his question had been so well deflected. Drosten still looked puzzled. In a few moments he was out-maneuvered again, as the older man contrived to ride beside Ivor, leaving Drosten with the younger one.

"I'm Eddarrnonn," the older man said, "tanist."

Ah! A Son of Irb, according to Drosten's story. Eddarmonn seemed old to be a tanist; his fighting days must be behind him now, but perhaps the hird had chosen him to be a restraining hand on the unusually young thane.

"Ivor of Glenbroch, sir." He did not mention that he served Mormaor Malcolm. And the best way to fight questions was with other questions. "How many swordsmen in the Glen Dorcha hird?"

"Hard to say. If you mean housecarls, who live here with their thane year-round, then no more than a dozen. But if you count all those who guard cattle in the hills in summer and drive them down to the glens in winter, then a lot more. Around two hundred of us rallied to the king's call in the Lothian campaign last summer. O' course some were mere bairns, but they fought like wolf cubs, I'm telling you."

And who had stayed behind to guard the kine? Just more "bairns"? The man's manner was odd, because most tanists would brag of the host their thane could raise, not belittle it. Glenbroch's hird was one of the largest in Malcolm's earldom, with its fleet alone needing one hundred fifty rowers. Malcolm had said that Elpin had a great many housecarls and crofters.

While Ivor was still trying to unravel that knot, Eddarmonn said, "The last time I saw a belt buckle like yours was down in Lothian. It was on a flaxen-haired youngster who rode into camp to report to the king."

"Sounds like Galan of Bragoran." Ivor knew it had been, since he'd sent Galan with that report. "He's the only blondie runner we've got." He wondered if Eddarrnonn had received the brains that Drosten had missed out on.

And the tanist wasn't done yet. "And I heard that the Northmen who arrived just in time to save your skins that day were brought there by one out of the same stable, a wee beardless bairn who yet wears the king's ring."

"Shouldn't believe everything you hear, sir," Ivor said. He might be beardless still, but his upper lip was fuzzy now, and he certainly wasn't wee.

Chapter 4

Thane Elpin's hall was long and narrow, but big, bigger even than the mormaor's hall at Stiegle. At that time of night it seemed dim and mysterious. It clearly served many purposes. Both weapons and farm tools hung on the walls, while the hearth in the center was furnished with several spits for roasting and stone hobs to hold pots. As was to be expected, this was where youths, male serfs, and unmarried housecarls slept, and many of both were already settling down on the floor for the night. Few seemed to be asleep yet, but on gloomy winter evenings there could be little to do except talk or tell tales. Ivor would have expected at least a minstrel, but perhaps one had already performed. The fire had been fed with wood to give light, so that white smoke billowed lazily overhead, seeking the smoke hole in the roof. Peats stacked nearby would be used to bank the blaze for the night.

Conversations stopped as the visitor was led along the length of the hall by housecarl Drosten and Tanist Eddarmonn—the other swordsman had stayed behind to see to the care of the horses. Eyes followed them, as if a stranger was a rarity in Glen Dorcha. Their destination was clearly a door at the far end, which surely led to the thane's private quarters, but those could not possibly be grand enough to make the place worthy of Lady Meg, at least not in Ivor's eyes. The first time he had seen Stiegle, he had been impressed, because it had seemed so much grander than Glenbroch. King Constantine's palace at Scone had impressed him even more. Compared to these Glen Dorcha was a desert and this hall a human stable. *Oh, Meg!*

Nowhere could be worthy of Meg.

The newcomers reached the door and halted. A few chinks of candlelight showed between planks, seeming bright in the gloom of the hall itself. Drosten rapped with his knuckles. There was a pause, and then some of the chinks went dark, and an angry voice on the far side growled: "Who is it?"

"Drosten, returned."

"With a runner bringing a message," Eddarmonn added.

"Just a moment." The darkened chinks brightened again as the speaker moved away from the door.

Two swordsmen and a runner waited in awkward silence. Ivor was amused that a thane would want to make himself respectable to meet a mere boy like him, but many men preferred to lie naked in their blankets, as he knew from his years of sleeping in the hall at Glenbroch, and a thane could afford as many fleeces and blankets as he wanted.

Then the chinks darkened again, the door opened, and a man slid out, closing it quickly behind him. Elpin was burly, with a bush of reddish beard and another, even redder and wilder, bush on his head, looking much in need of a comb. He wore a simple robe, with half the laces untied, and was currently shoeless.

Drosten and Ivor bowed. Eddarmonn had stepped back, out of the way.

"My lord, may I present Ivor of, um, Glenbroch," Drosten said, "captain of Earl Malcolm's runners?"

"Welcome, Ivor!" Elpin proclaimed in what might be called a hearty whisper. "Welcome to Dorcha! Welcome!" He clasped Ivor's shoulder and—to Ivor's astonishment—grabbed his hand to shake. "It must be a great honor to serve so splendid a lord in such an esteemed office as chief runner, and at such a tender age, too."

Unable to decide how to respond to that, Ivor mumbled something vague. A handshake was a greeting between equals, not between lord and boy. He was cruelly aware that his hand was soft from lack of sword practice, whereas the one gripping it was hard and rough as sandstone. And its grip was uncomfortably tight, too.

Elpin glanced aside as if noticing a signal, which must have come from Eddarmonn. The thane peered more closely at the hand he still held.

"But what is this on your thumb? Surely not the royal emblem? Come, let me see this better." Tightening his grip on Ivor's shoulder, the thane turned him around, and marched him back to the fire, the brightest place in the hall. It was nowhere near as bright as the room behind the door, though, so the purpose of this foolery must be to distract the visitor's notice from that. While Elpin made a show of examining the boar on the silver ring, Ivor glanced over his shoulder and saw a quick movement as someone emerged from that private place and disappeared into darkness. There had been no flash of light, so the candles inside had all been snuffed out. Just who had the thane been entertaining that he wanted kept secret?

"I am impressed!" Elpin at last released his hold on Ivor. "How did you earn this, young man? Malcolm... Nilcaster? They say that one of Malcolm's men saved the day at the battle of Nilcaster... a runner.... Was that you?"

THE RUNNER AND THE KELPIE

"I did no fighting, my lord. It was Earl Thorfinn and his horde who saved the day. I did arrive with them."

"That was not quite what I heard, but no matter, you must be weary after your journey, young friend Ivor. Steward? Steward!"

"Aye, my lord?" A man nearby rose, clutching his blanket around him.

"Bring meat and drink for my guest. Come, Ivor, let us retire and celebrate your arrival." He laid his heavy hand on Ivor's shoulder again and propelled him back the way they had come.

This was quite the oddest welcome Ivor had met in more than half a year of running. Anyone would think that he, not Malcolm, would determine who was to be Meg's husband. If it were, Thane Elpin would be out of the contest already, for there was something very shifty about him. Did false heartiness spring from a false heart?

The bedchamber was indeed now dark, and also insufferably hot for a man who had spent all day out in the cold damp of a Highland winter. Peat glowing on a stone hearth provided enough illumination for Elpin to locate a taper and then light half a dozen candles set in sconces around the walls. The room was larger than Ivor had expected, containing a bed big enough for two, a table, a couple of stools, a solid wood chest, and a curious second bed—a narrow bunk tucked in under a shelf laden with a miscellaneous heap of plates, clay beakers, bottles, a dagger, laundry, belts, spare candles, a tinderbox, and more. Possibly the thane's children had slept on the lower level while their mother was alive, and the upper level collected all the bric-a-brac of a rich man's life.

"Let me take your cloak, Ivor." Elpin lifted it off his shoulders, shook it, doubled it over, and threw it onto the spare bed. If he had hoped to hide the flimsy garment lying there, he failed. It was obviously nothing a man would wear, so now Ivor realized then what he should have guessed sooner: Elpin's mysterious companion earlier had been a woman. And this lecherous wretch thought he was worthy to marry Meg of Stiegle?

"Sit, lad, sit! You must be thirsty? Ah, there's a wee bit left in this jug." He filled a beaker and thrust it into Ivor's hand.

Ivor thanked him and drained it at a single long gulp. It was straight beer, which he disliked. No one dared drink water by itself, of course, unless it was taken right from a mountain spring. What he wanted most was fresh air, but the shutters were firmly closed, and the walls had been covered with leather to keep out drafts—they rippled as the wind blew, and no doubt in winter storms they would flap and slap against the timbers all night long. This was to be Meg's home for the rest of her life?

"So!" His host took a stool across the table from him and leaned forward eagerly. "How did your master like my offer, mm? He didn't send you all this way to say no, I'll wager."

Ivor stood up again, spread hands on thighs, and... and shivered as he felt a sudden surge of temptation, as if the Devil himself had whispered in his ear. He remembered what the Weird had prophesied, weeks ago. *"You will try to save a fair maiden."* Why not just say that Malcolm had other plans for his daughter?

No, no! He couldn't, he mustn't! He had sworn an oath to be true to Malcolm, to always repeat his words correctly. Besides, even if he did lie, Drosten would know that what he said wasn't true. Drosten would tell. And what could Ivor say when he went back? That Elpin had changed his mind? Gruoch had said Ivor would *try* to save a fair maiden. She hadn't said that the maiden was Meg, or that he would succeed in rescuing her. And he knew he wasn't even going to try.

Staring straight ahead, above Elpin's red mop he said, *"Earl Malcolm of Stiegle, Mormaor of the West, prince of Alba, admiral of the fleet, member of the king's council, lord of high justice, Thane of Invervuic, Thane of Bragoran, Thane of Ardenfort, et cetera, greets noble Thane Elpin of Glen Dorcha, saying: your offer for the hand of Meg, my daughter, is pleasing to my ears. My runner will proceed to Scone to advise His Grace of our intent, and seek his blessing on our negotiations. With His Grace's approval secured, you shall be most welcome to make all haste to Stiegle that we may embrace you and smooth the path to the happiness you seek. Thus spake Earl Malcolm."* Then he sat down.

"Great suffering sinners! Can you do that backwards too?" Then the big lout roared with laughter. "I'm only joking, Ivor. I am enormously impressed at the way you make that seem so easy. You can ride to Scone from here in a day, half a day in summer. And how will I know whether His Grace has given his consent? How soon will I be able to clasp my—"

He was interrupted by a rap on the door. He bellowed, "Enter!" In came the steward he had addressed earlier, bearing a laden tray. As he laid his burden on the table, the man took note of Ivor without meeting his eye and smiled a secret little smile, no doubt amused that his master's evening entertainment had been interrupted.

As the serf left, Ivor faced a heaped platter. No roast trout, alas, but a huge slab of cold meat, plus onions, bread, and cheese, making his mouth water so hard that it hurt. But he hadn't completed his duty yet.

"Earl Malcolm did give me permission to tell you his message to the king, my lord, and to return here with His Grace's reply before going on to Stiegle."

"Excellent!" Elpin hefted the jug and filled his own beaker before Ivor's. "Tell me, then."

Again Ivor stood up. *"Earl Malcolm of Stiegle greets his liege lord, Constantine II, by the Grace of God, King of the Scots and Picts, Lord of Alba, saying: I most humbly beg Your Grace's permission to discuss terms of a possible joining in matrimony of your noble Thane Elpin of Glen*

Dorcha and my daughter, including his offer to transfer title to the lands of Uachdar Moor to me, all subject to Your Grace's benign consent. Thus spake Earl Malcolm."

Ivor sat down and took out his eating knife. "He also instructed me that I might include your lordship's name in that, making it a joint appeal, should you so wish." He stuffed a thick wad of meat in his mouth before he could be asked any more questions.

"I'll have to hear it again, then, before I decide. But you eat your fill first, Ivor. You've had a long, hard ride. How was the weather on Uachdar?"

It took much longer than it should have done, because Elpin kept asking him things, but eventually Ivor felt full enough to release a loud belch of approval and lick his fingers. He watched uneasily as his host topped up his beaker yet again. This was much better beer than the first drink he had been offered. It seemed that guests were treated better than palace wenches, but his head was spinning.

He repeated the message to the king. Elpin announced that yes, he would like his name attached, and then demanded to hear what that would sound like. Of course it must sound quite different. Ivor managed to compose a joint appeal and recite it without stumbling, but only just. Fortunately Elpin saw his weariness at last and took mercy on him.

"And now I must let you rest, my young friend! You can sleep here." He rose and went to the second bed, scooping up Ivor's cloak and the other garment in one heap, which he dropped on the floor.

The bed certainly looked comfortable enough. Ivor could not refuse such an honor, of course, much as he would have preferred a corner of the hall, out with the housecarls and serfs. He had once slept in King Constantine's tent, but that had been in the field, during the war, and he had been almost out on his feet at the time. He had appreciated the king's merciful concern. Now he had a strange suspicion that Elpin just wanted to keep him under his own eye, so he couldn't pry or chatter with anyone else.

At the moment he had more urgent concerns, though. "That is most gracious of you, my lord. I must first make a brief visit to the pits."

"Oh, don't bother with that," the thane said. "Just open yon shutter and aim at the moon."

Chapter 5

Ivor emerged from the hall the next morning to find blue sky. The sun was still below the eastern hills, but obviously the day was to be a fine one. Gawkie might think that he deserved a rest after yesterday's long trek, but he was going to go and eat the king's oats in Scone whether he wanted to or not.

A few mangy dogs sniffed the stranger suspiciously, but did not venture to express any opinions about him. He could hear hounds squabbling somewhere on the far side of the hall, also horses and cattle making their mournful calls in the distance. One late-rising rooster was still calling for his wives. Women were coming back from the well with buckets of water or carrying laundry to the river. The day smelled good.

By daylight Dorcha was an even poorer excuse for a village than it had seemed in the night: turf hovels in a sea of mud. Seen from outside, the hall itself looked old and ramshackle, its log walls mossy and even rotting in places, the chinking falling out. Its roof sagged. Above the door hung a board with a curious design of a beast on it: a horse? a dolphin? a monster out of some artist's nightmares? Meg's nightmares to be?

"It's a rare day for a ride, friend Ivor," announced Thane Elpin, right behind him. "You'll ha' nay trouble making Scone before nightfall."

"Only if I don't get lost, my lord. Can someone come with me to put me on the right road?"

"Och, it's no trouble at all. Just go down along the loch until you get to the river. Follow that, and it'll take you right to the Tatha itself. You'll know the way, then, won't you, you being a bearer of the king's ring?"

Ivor agreed that he would be able to follow the Tatha River to Scone, but he was convinced now that there was a plot afoot to keep him from talking to anyone in Glen Dorcha other than the thane, the tanist, and the trusted Drosten. Sure enough, Elpin himself escorted him to the horse paddock and saw that the grooms there brought him his horse and tack. He ordered trail rations brought for his saddlebag. And finally he shook Ivor's hand again, wished him safe journey and quick return, and watched him ride away.

▶▼◀

Glen Dorcha was a fine enough place if you liked naked scenery. No doubt the hills would blush prettily with heather in the spring, and they did have patches of real forest in places. The bottomland offered good pasture and some cultivation, its fields outlined by dry stone dykes. But winter would be bleak indeed, with snow, rather than the rain that Meg was used to. Ivor knew, because Rorie of Ytter had told him so, that Stiegle was not much by the standards of Christendom—not Rome or Jerusalem, or the Saxons' burghs in Wessex—but it was a lot better than this.

So what, he pondered as he rode to the loch, was being

hidden from his view here? Why had he been given no chance to look around or meet with more of the inhabitants?

Malcolm had warned him the marriage negotiations must be kept secret, and perhaps that was excuse enough, although surely Elpin must know that an earl's runner could be trusted not to gossip. When Ivor had arrived at the thane's door last night and Drosten had announced his return, the quicker-witted Eddarmonn had added a warning that he had brought a runner, as a hint that Elpin had better hide his companion. Again, that had been a reasonable precaution—if you must have sex out of wedlock, don't let your future father-in-law hear about it.

Ivor decided he didn't like Glen Dorcha. He didn't like its thane. He knew he would never like any man who was going to marry Meg of Stiegle, but there was something about Elpin that repelled him. He had been far too effusive, treating Ivor as a long-lost friend instead of a servant. He was new to his title, of course, but not so new that he hadn't led his hird on the king's invasion of Lothian in the summer. He should be accustomed to respect and dignity by now.

He had lost his father, his lord, and his wife in... how long? Ivor didn't know. What sort of a curse besieged a man with such sorrows and yet promoted him to thane?

▶▼◀

Soon Ivor came to the marshy shores of the loch and the trail divided. Scone lay on the left bank of the Tatha. If the Dorcha River was a tributary, as Elpin had said, then he had better not follow the low road around the loch, because if he couldn't find somewhere to cross the Dorcha, he would find himself trapped on the wrong side of it when he reached the Tatha. He turned Gawkie to what Dorsten had called the high road.

It was worse than he had expected, and even the sure-footed Gawkie had trouble. The trail went up and down, in places skirting the lake and in others climbing about two hundred feet up the slope. Sometimes it slanted to the side—quite often a surface of bare, slippery rock slanting toward a vertical drop; sometimes it crossed long cones of scree that had fallen from the cliffs above. The glen must have other exits farther up, for no one could drive cattle out at this end unless the loch froze solid.

When boy and horse at last descended to the lowland where the Dorcha River had its source, Ivor wiped the sweat from his eyes and patted Gawkie's neck. "Never again," he promised, "will I put you through that. When we come back we'll go in by the low road again, I swear."

▶▼◀

After that, though, they made good progress and it was barely noon when they started up the hill to the king's palace. With the land at peace again, there were only token guards on the gate, and Ivor rode unchallenged into the tangle of buildings within the wall. He knew his way around well enough to find the stable without trouble, and his boar ring was enough to have the hands saluting him and promising to pamper his horse. They also assured him that King Constantine was in residence, not off hunting somewhere, as he might well be at this time of year, for weeks at a time.

As always after a long ride, Ivor felt that he had shrunk when he set off on his own two feet. The palace seemed quieter than he ever remembered it, but that might be because his previous visits had been during the preparations for the Lothian campaign or in the wind-down period after it. The best place to look for the king was the Reception Hall, which was a freestanding building near the centre of the maze. Two guards in the porch jumped to their feet when he approached, but he was unarmed and again his buckle and his ring worked magic. They greeted him by name, and cheerfully exchanged blessings with him as he strode in through the open door.

The anteroom within took up most of the building. A row of a dozen or so stools in the centre were all empty, but the benches against the walls held about a score of people. Their presence told him at once that Constantine was undoubtedly behind that imposing door at the far end. He headed for that, aware of all the disapproving looks he was receiving as he went by, for those who recognized his runner's badge would worry that he might take precedence over them, and the rest would assume he was a boy who didn't belong in grownups' affairs.

At a small deck sat an elderly ostiary, one Ivor had not met before. His tonsure showed that he was a cleric, and his robe that he was a Benedictine monk. He looked up sourly at this juvenile intruder, but his expression warmed slightly when he recognized the emblem of a Stiegle runner. Then Ivor flashed his ring at him and the man reached at once for his chalk and slate.

"Runner Ivor, sent by Earl Malcolm. No, wait," Ivor added as the ostiary rose. "Pray do not interrupt His Grace. My business is not urgent." His ring would override almost anything.

The man's eyebrows rose in astonishment, but he settled back on his stool. "As you wish, Runner."

Ivor turned to look over the lines of petitioners on the benches. Most of them were finely dressed in wool and fur, some were dignified and gray-bearded, others brawny young fighters, a couple of them churchmen, none of them women. All of them were still regarding the newcomer with disapproval. No doubt some had been there since dawn, but the king was under no obligation to see them in the order of their arrival, or to see them at all. After each audience ended, he would listen as the ostiary read over his list and choose the one he would see next. Those still remaining at the end of the day might be told to return tomorrow and try again—or might not.

Ivor recognized only one of them. One of the fighting toughs had risen and was grinning ferociously at him through a stubbly red-gold beard. He was hatless and sported a matching red-gold ponytail and Ivor was already halfway to meet him.

They collided into an embrace that squashed all the air out of his lungs, followed by some enthusiastic shoulder-thumping that made Ivor's knees buckle and left his fist sore. Rorie played with hammers and anvils in his spare time and was built like an oak tree. He was also decked out with more gold and jewellery than anyone else in the room: bracelets, rings on fingers and in ears.

"Hell's cinders! You're *still* growing!"

"Guano I am. You're shrinking, old man."

They grinned at each other, ignoring the audience outraged by such unseemly behaviour—practically in the king's presence, too! They sat down on stools, knee to knee.

"You're quite a hero now, laddie. And still doing well at your running, I see. You're not the green bairn I sent to Stiegle."

"Just lucky. What're you doing over here in the east? Hiding out from jealous husbands, I suppose?"

"Fallen on hard times, begging for crusts."

"I can see that you're dressed in rags. Very good quality rags, though."

Rorie of Ytter was a sellsword. He had led a troop of his own hirelings at the Battle of Nilcaster and won much praise from Malcolm, who was rumoured to have offered him a high position in his own hird, but Rorie always preferred to remain his own man. Before he could respond to Ivor's scorn, his attention wandered to something behind Ivor's back.

Ivor spun around to see. The door to the Presence Chamber had swung open, and a man wearing fancy robes and a bishop's mitre came striding out, his face scarlet with rage. Most of the waiting petitioners slid off their benches and knelt to receive his blessing, but he stormed past them without a glance. Ivor would have knelt or at least bowed, but Rorie made no move to rise, so he didn't, either. His Reverence vanished out the door, closely followed by the two clerics.

"Mm," Rorie said with amusement. "That's the third man to come out yowling with his tail between his legs. I think I may slink away and return tomorrow, when His Grace may be in a better mood."

But Ivor wouldn't. If the king was indeed in a bad temper today, he might straightway forbid any talk of marriage between Meg and Elpin, which would be fine by the runner, despite the fact that he was not supposed to have any opinion on the matter.

But then there was a collective gasp. The ostiary had disappeared into the Presence Chamber, but it was the king himself who emerged to scan the hall. Everyone lurched to their feet to bow.

"Ivor!" he called. "Ivor of Glenbroch! Come here, lad, and let's have a look at you."

Even Rorie's eyes stretched wide.

"Gotta go," Ivor murmured. "A friend needs me."

Rorie said, "Thor's knuckles!"

Chapter 6

Ivor had no chance even to bow before the king seized his arm and hauled him through the doorway. "Send in lunch for myself and this man," he told the ostiary over his shoulder. "Double for him. He eats like starving horses." He slammed the door.

Constantine son of Áed was in his twenties, and in all Ivor's dealings with him, had seemed a quiet-spoken, earnest young man, almost like a junior cleric; although he did not seem to be lettered, for when Ivor had brought him documents, Constantine had always sent for a churchman to read them to him. He had his face shaven regularly, keeping only a trim mustache, and he dressed simply. He did not look like a warrior, yet he had been successful in war so far, and had just demonstrated how he could squelch even bishops.

The audience chamber was quite small, and its only real sign of luxury was glass in the window, coloured to prevent anyone seeing in. Even the throne was just a wooden chair with a cushion on the seat and a canopy above it, although there must be a much grander one somewhere in the palace. The walls were hung with tapestries, and in one place a drape that likely concealed another exit. A crucifix hung above a fireplace presently unlit; four simple stools and a table completed the furnishings.

If Constantine had indeed been in a bad mood when he received the previous three petitioners, he showed no sign of it now. He laughed. "You are a welcome sight, young Ivor! I am surrounded by pompous, greedy, half-witted ne'er-do-wells, and I know you are none of those." He looked Ivor up and down, but he never made jokes about his height. "I believe you're starting to put some meat on your bones."

"Your Grace is kind."

"Not often. How well do you know that man you were talking with out there?"

"Rorie of Ytter? I know him quite well, Your Grace." Suddenly Ivor saw a pit yawning before him. He liked to think of Rorie as a friend. It had been through Rorie that Ivor had met Malcolm and been hired as a runner. And it had been partly because of Ivor that Malcolm had lifted a sentence of death on Rorie. But loyalty to the king must come even before friendship. "He is a great fighter, but he.... He can be a dangerous helper, sire."

The king nodded, satisfied. So he already knew of the terrible curse that Rorie bore, and Ivor need not spell it out.

"As long as you're aware. Come over here." The king led the way to the table and sat down. He looked up expectantly.

"So, Ivor-me-lad. You told the monk that your business isn't important? You realize that no one else in all Alba would ever say that? Every one of those avaricious brickheads out there insists that I must see him immediately on matters of extreme urgency."

"I believe I told him that the matter was not *urgent*, Your Grace. My lord's business is always important to me."

THE RUNNER AND THE KELPIE

"Good. Let's hear it then."

Ivor came to attention and repeated the spiel he had composed the previous evening.

"Earl Malcolm of Stiegle and Thane Elpin of Glen Dorcha greet their liege lord, Constantine II, by the Grace of God, King of the Scots and Picts, Lord of Alba, saying: we most humbly beg Your Grace's permission to discuss terms of a possible joining in matrimony of the aforesaid thane and Margaret, daughter of the aforesaid earl, including the thane's offer to transfer title to the lands of Uachdar Moor to the earl, all subject to Your Grace's benign consent. Thus spake Earl Malcolm and Thane Elpin."

Silence. The king was frowning. Then came a tap at the door and he said, "Go and let them in."

"Them" turned out to be a solitary page younger than Ivor, carrying a laden tray. He laid it on the table, bowed, and was given a nod of dismissal. He closed the door behind him.

The tray bore three meat pies, steaming and leaking gravy; bread and cheese; onions; and a bowl of hard-boiled eggs. Eggs at this time of year were a rare treat. Ivor's mouth was watering already, but the king was thinking of something other than food.

At last he said, "Have Malcolm and Elpin met?"

A runner should not be asked questions outside the text of his message, but kings were special. "No, sire. The thane sent a housecarl to Stiegle with the offer, and I went back with him to Glen Dorcha to deliver the earl's reply."

"Mph. And what does the lady herself think of the match?"

Ivor gulped. That one was definitely out of bounds! "I don't know the answer to that, sire."

The king looked at him doubtfully. "You can't even guess?"

Ivor just shook his head. It certainly was not his job to feed the king on his own guesswork.

"Even if Malcolm hasn't met Elpin, you have. What did you think of him?"

What did Ivor's opinion matter? But this was his chance! *You will try to rescue a fair maiden.* The king was asking for his honest opinion, and even if he was only being gracious and polite to a messenger, Ivor could answer truthfully without being unfaithful to Malcolm. "I... I didn't like him, sire. I'm not sure why. You know how a dog sniffs at a stranger and sometimes its hackles rise? That's the effect Thane Elpin had on me—Your Grace."

The king nodded solemnly, as if this in any way mattered. "And what of the thane's allegiance? Is that on the table?"

There were meat pies on the table, damn it! But that was the question Ivor had foreseen.

"It believe it has been mentioned, Your Grace."

"Mph. What did Malcolm say about it?"

What Malcolm had said was that the king would choke on the idea.

"I was not present when it was discussed, Your Grace."

Constantine frowned. "Sit down and eat. I need to think about this."

Needing no second command, Ivor sat, pulled out his knife, and set to work. Constantine paced back and forth a few times, then settled on his throne and stared at nothing for a while, drumming fingers on one knee. The prospects for Thane Elpin's suit did not look good, which was excellent news for Ivor.

Eventually Constantine came and joined him at the table, but he barely nibbled at his meal. "I suppose I could eat like you if I ran sixty miles a day."

"I can't run that far in a day, sire!"

"I've known you to come close." The king smiled. "I admire your stamina, and I also admire your tact and judgment. Whenever I ask you something I shouldn't—and I do that to all messengers, not just you—your replies are very carefully worded. Sometimes I can read the answer in your face, but not very often. And now I've made you blush again, and I'm sorry." He pushed the third meat pie across to Ivor.

Ivor kept his head down and gobbled it up. When he had cleaned his platter, if not quite filled his belly, he wondered briefly if it would rude to offer to finish the king's pie, and decided it would be. So he licked his fingers, then wiped and sheathed his knife.

He jumped to his feet when the king said, "Ready?"

"Aye, Your Grace."

"First a message to the mormaor alone, on another matter. Informal titles. *The king to Earl Malcolm: After further consideration, I am still inclined to support the proposal made by Bishop Pol. His plan seems most promising, but let me know if you decide against it.*

"Secondly, as to the message that you brought, I'm going to give you one reply addressed to both. Usual titles for all three. Hear my words: *For us to approve the union you propose would cause a drastic change in the balance of power in our kingdom, and therefore we require that you justify it in person to our council when next it meets, here in Scone, on Candlemas Day.*"

So thorough had Ivor's training been that he memorized even short messages without understanding the words. In this case he had repeated the whole text back to the king before the meaning registered. It went farther than his wildest hopes. *The king did not approve of the match!* He had not directly forbidden it, but from a monarch such a broad hint was an edict. Surely Malcolm and Elpin must break off negotiations after hearing that message! Meg was saved from Glen Dorcha, at least until Candlemas Day, the second of February, and almost certainly forever.

Then he saw the king watching him wryly and wondered if he had been leering like a stupid dolphin.

"How's your horse?" the king asked with a smile.

Ivor's mind was still turning cartwheels. "Horse, Your Grace?"

"You're wearing shoes, so you rode in."

"Oh. I think he's able enough yet, Your Grace." If Ivor returned to Dorcha tonight, he could be in Stiegle tomorrow, passing on the good news to Meg.

"Then be on your way with my blessing," said the king. "And my messages."

He bowed and withdrew. The ostiary rose and took his list in to the king.

Ivor strode through the audience chamber unseeing and was almost at the door when he found Rorie barring his way, and this time he knew he must have been grinning like an idiot, because Rorie was.

"I see that His Grace favours beanpole runners over bishops today."

'This one, maybe."

"You look as if he just gave you a county." But Rorie knew that he would not be told what had been discussed.

"We've been trading funny stories."

The ostiary came marching out to summon the next petitioner. "Freeman Rorie of Ytter!" he proclaimed in a voice like a rooster's morning scream.

"Ah," Rorie said, "A friend needs me."

To which Ivor could only mutter, "Thor's elbows?"

THE RUNNER AND THE KELPIE

Chapter 7

Ivor almost ran to the stable. There he flashed his ring and the hands jumped to saddle Gawkie for him; he was free to lean against a doorpost and grin at the universe. Malcolm would have to find a worthier husband for his daughter, although where could he possibly start looking?

Gawkie wasn't happy at the prospect of yet another journey, but made a lot less trouble than someone his size could have. Ivor rode down to the Tatha and turned upstream. He passed gangs of serfs bringing in the last of the harvest and others repairing a dry stone dyke. They all waved to the king's man, and he waved back without seeing them. Partridges shot up from the grass, startling Gawkie, and his rider calmed him and rode on as if nothing had happened—and had any one asked, he would have said that nothing had. He was too happy to notice such distractions. Meg was saved from a life sentence in Glen Dorcha with that smarmy, backslapping thane. Thanks be to God!

Had that been because of Ivor's insolent remark about

hackles? Had that opinion rescued the maiden, or just confirmed the king in what he would have decided anyway?

At the same time, he regretted that he had not been able to tarry and gossip with Rorie. After the best part of two days on the road, he could have justified a rest period for both himself and Gawkie. Most people never went anywhere outside their home glen, but Rorie travelled all the time and always had good tales to tell. Why, after earning praise from Malcolm during the summer campaign, had he come east to call on the king? Why was he not already shut up in his winter hermitage at Ytter, forging more of his incomparable swords?

The king had known of the curse on him, so perhaps he knew of one on Elpin also? Father, lord, and wife in quick succession? Could that be why Constantine had basically banned the marriage? He might have spared Meg even more misfortune than Ivor had foreseen.

▶▼◀

As the day began to fade, so did the effect of the meat pies he had eaten, and he began to think that spending the night in Scone would have been a wiser course. Clouds were building in the west, promising rain. He was returning by the same path he had followed in the morning, along the left bank of the Dorcha River, so unless he could ford it, he would have to risk the horrible high road again.

When he reached the loch, the sun had already gone behind the clouds, but he could see that the river had shrunk a lot, even since that morning, so he pointed Gawkie at the ford. Gawkie was understandably reluctant to enter that cold brown water, sliding over its bed of slippery, cobble-sized rocks, but he let himself be persuaded, and crossed without mishap.

The next decision was whether to risk the low road through the trees or head up the slope to the shelter that Drosten had pointed out, and overnight there. The moon, just into its second quarter, was already high in the sky and would provide some light just by shining off the lake. This time it was Gawkie who made the decision, because he didn't know about the shelter and he did remember the trail. He also remembered oats and a rubdown last night, so he plodded wearily over to the start of the forest path.

A ramshackle board hung on the first real tree. Ivor did not recall seeing it the previous day, but it looked as if it had been there a long time, and the shape drawn on the wood, although badly weathered, was the same as the sign on the thane's hall, a strange unworldly beastie. It must represent his personal sign, like the king's boar and Malcolm's running horse; Ivor made a note to ask about it in the morning. He chuckled as he recalled that Constantine's men used his emblem as a battle cry, "The boar! The boar!" He doubted that a squad of swordsmen charging across a battlefield shouting, "The beastie! The beastie!" would be nearly as awesome.

Moon or not, it was very dark in among the trees. Rocks and tree roots made the footing uncertain, so Gawkie slowed down even more, testing every step. There was no point in pushing him and risking a sprained fetlock, so Ivor endured in patience until the dumb animal finally stopped altogether and tried to turn around, which was very unlike him. When Ivor insisted, he went a few more steps, then balked again. Ivor kicked him and cursed him. Together they progressed a few yards at a time.

"Stupid, stubborn, half-witted, worthless plug! Move, or we'll be here all night!"

Faced with that choice, Gawkie seemed to conclude that staying there all night would be preferable to taking one more step, and all his rider's insults weren't going to change his small but determined mind. Ivor sat there on Gawkie's back, helpless, in a gloom that was very close to complete darkness now. Right in front of him was a place where the path dipped almost to water level, and the ground became marshy. The screen of trees and shrubbery between it and the lake was very narrow. He could hear the water lapping the shore just a few feet to his right, and heavy raindrops hitting the leaves high overhead. He could feel his horse shivering. What could possibly be upsetting him so much?

The wind was rising as the storm drew closer. The lapping of the ripples grew louder, the light from the water fainter. Maybe he should let his horse be the judge, and go back? But there would be nothing to eat in that little kennel on the hillside, and it was a long time since those meat pies.

He wished he had a riding crop, or spurs. He did have his belt knife, which had a sharp point, but he couldn't bring himself to treat a poor dumb animal so. Besides, if the unexpected pain panicked him, the results might be dangerous. Just how dangerous Ivor discovered when there came a huge splashing sound from the lake, as if someone or something were wallowing there: coming ashore, perhaps? Gawkie emitted a scream of terror and bolted.

Ivor threw himself flat along the horse's outstretched neck to avoid low branches that could blind or stun him, and braced himself for disaster. The horse was blundering, stumbling, terrified out of his wits by... something. He could not possibly race through the forest in darkness, and the wild ride did not last long, although longer than Ivor had expected. Gawkie shot across the low, marshy spot, plunged into the denser forest beyond, then went down with a crash, sending Ivor cartwheeling into the trees.

He cried out in pain. The impact dazed him, and for a moment he couldn't decide where he hurt most, only that it would be easier to count the places where he didn't. *Stupid, stupid, stupid!* Now, far too late, he realized what that notice board meant.

Back before his mother died, when he was the baby of the brood and there were only three of them left at home—he and Lachlan and Neil—then sometimes Fergus, who was fourteen or fifteen and supposed to be sleeping in the hall, would creep back at night whenever their mother was out assisting at a birth or a funeral, and he would scare the wee uns out of their wits with ghost stories, and tales of monsters. The worst monsters were kelpies. Kelpies lived in lochs and streams and preyed on travellers, dragging them into the water to drown them or eat them. They could take any shape, usually that of a horse, but sometimes of a woman.

So that was what the board meant: it was a warning of a kelpie. Why else would the shelter have been put so far from the loch? *And Weird Gruoch had warned him that he would meet the monster of his dream!*

He took stock of his damage. Face bleeding, ribs, right arm, left ankle... *Ooo-yi-yi!* Especially left ankle. But he hadn't lost any eyes or teeth. Poor Gawkie had done worse, for Ivor could hear him whimpering with fear and struggling to stand up, but he wasn't managing that, so he'd probably broken a leg or two. And then, more distant, there came a strange snuffling, snorting noise, something breathing. Something *very big* breathing.

Then came crunching, swishing noises—the sort of noise something large might make if it were forcing its way through that thin screen of shrubbery where Gawkie had panicked. In most places the trees were thick enough to form a fence between the path and the loch, but not there.

Ivor was on his feet.... *Ooo-yi-yi!* again. He was on one foot. If he hadn't broken his left ankle, he'd sprained it badly, and his right shoulder hurt like hellfire, too. The kelpie continued to snuffle, coming closer. It was ashore now, he was certain, ashore and following his trail, so the disabled Gawkie lay between them, but Ivor wasn't going to rely on that barrier being enough to save him. He had no light and no weapon other than his belt knife.

At least he wasn't tied to a tree, as he had been in the nightmare. Could he climb one? In daylight, maybe, but the woods were so deep and the trunks so close together that very few had branches low enough for him to reach. He crouched down and felt all around him for a stick that he might use as a cane. The first one he found was old and rotten; it snapped in his hands. So he stood up again, unsteadily, and began to hobble on one foot along the path, using the trees as support when he had to hop. His progress was slow and painful.

Gawkie screamed again, and then again; there were sounds of wood breaking, followed by much splashing, and it was easy to imagine the poor beast being dragged into the lake to drown. But would the kelpie be satisfied with horse meat?

Ivor continued to struggle along the path, weeping with both pain and fear. Then his hands found a slender sapling that would be light enough to use as a staff. He took out his knife to cut it, but that was easier thought than done. Although he kept his knife sharp, it was no wood saw, and he had to whittle slices off, which wasn't easy in the dark while standing on one foot. Eventually he managed to snap the weakened stem. Struggling, he fumbled his hands up its length until he thought he could snap off the top, whose twigs and leaves would undoubtedly catch in the other trees and impede him.

After that, he managed to make a little better progress, clutching his staff in both hands, holding his left foot high to avoid banging it on anything... but oh, still so slow! If the kelpie had managed to drag the crippled horse out through the undergrowth to the lake, then it could certainly come ashore again there and follow Ivor. Or, of course, it might go on up the loch until it found a wider gap, an easier access. And in that case, it would be ahead of him, waiting for him.

He said several prayers.

The wind and rain were still growing stronger, making it harder to hear anything else, even those bloodcurdling snuffling noises he had heard earlier. He should probably have turned back when he heard the kelpie dragging poor old Gawkie off, because the thane's hall remained very far away; he was still much closer to the beginning than the end of the path.

Then his right foot slid on a slight slope and came down in water, so he only saved his balance by setting down his injured foot and the stab of pain made him cry out. He caught a glimpse of the lake through a parting in the trees and realized that he'd found one of the little burns that fed the loch; it was wide but very shallow, more mud than water. He'd forgotten that the trail dipped several times to cross such streams or boggy patches. The kelpie might come ashore in any of these without making any noise at all. It might already be ahead of him! And how many of these dips had Drosten and he crossed? Five? Six? He couldn't possibly keep up this hobbling all the way to the settlement. He should have gone back.

He should never have entered the forest at dusk, but it was too late to change that.

Not far away from him, in the direction he was heading, a horse whinnied. Ivor's heart leaped into his throat. He stopped where he was and tried to decide what to do. If that was just a trick, he ought to keep going. But if the kelpie was now in front of him, he ought to go back. And the night was young—it could probably play with him for hours, until he was unable to move at all. Or could there be two kelpies?

More whinnying, and in a moment he saw something moving in the darkness ahead of him. Something white. Something big, very big. Perhaps his imagination was deceiving him, but he thought it was horse-like, a pale horse, so he could sense its shape even in the deep gloom. It was also very large. It whinnied again and tossed its mane.

"No!" he yelled, as loud as he could. "Go away, demon!" He shouted out a prayer and drew his knife. What a pathetic weapon against such a ghoul!

"?" the horse whickered, and clumped a pace forward, its great feet splashing in the water. It lowered its head and snuffled some very horsey noises—offering a free ride, of course. If it really was a horse, Ivor was saved. He could clamber on its back and ride it all the way to the hall, for warmth and food and a blanket.... *Stop that!* It wasn't real. It was the kelpie. It would carry him off into the loch and drown him.

Gruoch had prophesied that he would refuse help when it was offered. He stepped back up, out of the stream. *Splash, splash*... the kelpie was following. He found a tree trunk to lean against, thick enough that it did not bend, and raised his staff like a lance in both hands. In his dream he had been tied to a tree with rope. Now he wasn't tied, but he might as well be.

"You come any closer, I'll bang your eyes out!"

The kelpie whinnied sadly. Then, suddenly, it moved and wasn't there any more. Water splashed. Waves splashed around his foot. Ivor blinked, but the monster had definitely gone. What sort of trickery was this? Was it just going to wait until he was even more exhausted, and then return with its offer of a ride on its back? Did he struggle on, through this stream, and try to keep going? Or, should he perhaps crawl into the trees, up the hill? He would have to go on hands and knees, over rocks and roots, through thorns and brambles, but he was much skinnier than the kelpie, wasn't he? Maybe not, because the kelpie could change shape. Well, if he got far enough away from the lake...?

"Ivor? Ivor of Glenbroch!"

The voice was distant, but familiar, and it came from behind him. Could a kelpie speak? Could it take not just human form, but the form of a particular person? He didn't know, but he might be about to find out.

A light was coming, flickering between tree trunks, and held high, as if by a man on horseback. Ivor could hear the hooves, chinking on stones, splashing in damp patches. He had never realized that it was possible to be so scared and still live....

"Ivor!" The light came into view and halted.

"Where's your horse, man? Why're you standing on one leg? If you're hoping I'll mistake you for a heron, I don't like your chances."

Even worse! "No!" Ivor screamed. "Go away! I don't want to be rescued by you! I will *not* be rescued by you!"

Chapter 8

"I don't believe you've got much choice," said Rorie of Ytter, "because I am going to rescue you whether you want me to or not, and I'm bigger than you are. Well, broader and thicker. You have a yard or two on me in height, I'll admit."

"No. I'll be cursed. Your curse will get me."

"It won't, because you haven't *asked* me to help you. In fact you are begging me *not* to help you, so that's all right. If I get down off this nag, will you please put that knife away?"

"Dismount first." Ivor could believe that the kelpie might take other shapes, but surely only one at a time? Even a man *on* a horse, perhaps. But not a man *and* a horse....

Rorie chuckled, swung his leg up, and slid out of the saddle. Then he laid his lantern down while he tied Hillrunner's reins to a tree. Yes, Ivor knew that roan gelding. Then he could accept that this really was Rorie of Ytter, who was armed with a sword and knew how to use it, so Ivor of Glenbroch really was saved. He sheathed his knife.

He said another prayer.

"Oh, Rorie.... I'm sorry I doubted you!" Ivor reminded himself sternly that heroes never burst into tears when being rescued. He managed not to; wasn't easy.

Rorie brought the lantern close. "You're a mess, lad. Anything broken?"

"I think my ankle's just sprained. My ribs hurt a bit."

"We're safe now. Kelpies never attack men in groups, and I've got a fair-to-middling sword arm. Can you ride? Let's get you on Hillrunner, and I'll walk."

He untied the roan and brought him closer, and Ivor realized that he must put his left foot in the stirrup to mount, and then lean his weight on his chest... *Dear God, give me strength!* But it was Rorie of Ytter who gave him strength, for when Ivor raised his foot, Rorie hooked an arm under his thigh and heaved him bodily up, into the saddle. Although he managed it without screaming aloud, his face was running sweat and he thought he had bitten his lip again.

"That was nobly done," Rorie murmured, looking up at him. "Here, have a drink. If you feel faint at all and need a break, just say so. Falling off won't help one bit."

"I'm fine," Ivor lied. But he recognized the taste of water sweetened with palace beer, and it helped rid his mouth of blood.

Holding the lantern in one hand and Hillrunner's reins in the other, Rorie set off along the path, heading for the hall. "You needn't keep twisting your head around. The kelpie won't trouble us. If it comes anywhere near us, Hillrunner will warn us."

"Wouldn't it be quicker to go back to that shelter?" Ivor muttered. He had bitten his tongue, too.

"It would, but we'd arrive soaked, with no fire and not much chance of starting one. I'm frozen and I think you are, too." He was being polite; it was reaction to terror that was making Ivor shiver like an aspen leaf. "What happened to your horse?"

"The kelpie spooked him, so he bolted. He fell and broke a leg, I think. Then it dragged him away, poor fellow. Why were you following me?"

"Wasn't. Not specifically. I was heading for Glen Dorcha. I knew you were ahead of me, because the king said so, and I saw you fording the river, but I was still too far away to shout. Couldn't believe my eyes when I saw you ride into the woods, right past the kelpie warning."

"I'm a salt water bairn. We don't have those nasty kelpie things in Stiegle or Glenbroch."

Rorie waded through one of the dips without hesitation, and Hillrunner followed calmly enough. It must be true that the kelpie only preyed on solitary travellers.

"You have selkies, don't you—seal women? They must be even worse. Anyway, I rode up to the shelter because I remembered that there had been a lantern there when I looked in it once. Lucky it was still there, and oil too, or I think I'd have let the beastie have you. Coming along here in the dark is plain suicide."

Rorie had been everywhere and knew everything, of course. But Rorie didn't always tell the truth.

"If you're going to Glen Dorcha for the dancing and wild parties," Ivor said, "I think you'll be disappointed."

"I'm going because the king told me too. He's heard some curious rumours about the place."

"He knows about your curse, doesn't he?"

"Oh, yes. See, that was a very nice little war you won for us, Warrior Ivor, but it wasn't too profitable. I got some nice fighting in for Malcolm, both before Nilcaster and in the big brouhaha there. Constantine got his Lothian lands back, but your friend Thorfinn took most of the movable loot home with him and most of the able-bodied prisoners, too. I couldn't find any other fights going on, so I took service with the king. He pays me and gives me *orders*. He doesn't *ask* me to do anything for him, so the curse doesn't apply."

They had come to another wet dip, and Rorie stopped talking for a moment while they forded it.

"And in case you're wondering, I just got back from the north and was waiting to give him my report on a mess I uncovered up there, when you walked into the anteroom. He called me in right after you—remember?—and told me to head up to Glen Dorcha and.... Just a moment."

He thrust the reins into Ivor's hands and backed up a few paces. Then he crouched down to examine the ground, moving the lantern from side to side. His broad back hid whatever he was doing, but in a moment he stood up, drew his sword, and cut a long slice of bark off the nearest tree. Then he took the reins back and resumed the journey.

Why? Ivor didn't ask. He was past caring. Thoughts of that warm hall and a blanket consumed him. A hay pallet would be even nicer, but a bed of shingle would do....

▶ ▼ ◀

He almost went to sleep before reaching the hall. Several times he was so close to it that he began to slide off the horse, then a jab of pain from his bruises would waken him just in time. He was aware when they came to the end of the forest, because then the rain could get at them. It seemed a long time before they drew close enough to the hall for the dogs to start barking.

Then there were angry voices, one of which he recognized as belonging to Eddarrnonn, the tanist. Another was certainly Rorie's. Rainwater was running down Ivor's neck. Then a hand reached up to grab his chin and Thane Elpin's hairy face loomed close in the torchlight.

"What did the king say?"

"Huh?"

"The king. You went to see the king, what did he say, yes or no?"

"Said no," Ivor mumbled. The thane swore and disappeared.

His protests were ignored as he was dragged out of the saddle and carried into the hall. Men poked up the peat fire to get more heat out of it as others hauled his clothes off. Sleepy voices complained of noise and lighted torches. Strong beer, tasted good. Someone had fetched a big woman named Bula, who seemed to be the village healer, and she washed his face and felt his ribs—*ow!*—and ankle with hands rough as millstones. It was all shameful, but he was too weary to argue. Finally they rolled him up in blankets and let him sleep; which was not as easy as he expected, but gradually the normal hall snoring chorus picked up and he drifted away.

Chapter 9

Morning was bad, because he urgently needed to run outside and attend to a call of nature, but how could he even stand without help? He did manage to sit up—painfully—and look around. He identified the nearest bundle as Rorie, from the red hair showing at one end, but he was still asleep. Other men were moving, though, and one young man in need of a haircut came over, carrying a couple of poles. He wasn't much older than Ivor, just old enough to be a housecarl.

He dropped to one knee and offered a hand. "Taran son of Ciniod."

"Ivor of Glenbroch." The handshake was a reminder that Ivor had skinned his palms by grabbing trees while trying to run away from the kelpie on one foot.

"Thought you might need these," Taran said. "My dad made them for me when I broke a leg last year. They're likely a wee bit short for you." The poles were rough-trimmed branches, each ending in a fork that had been padded with rags to support a man's armpit.

"Much better than nothing. Thanks."

With Taran's help Ivor rose and found his balance on the crutches, standing on one bare foot and dangling a bandaged one. He was wearing a bare minimum, mostly gooseflesh, so Taran wrapped his blanket around him and then guided him outside to attend to his morning problem. Rain was falling, which was a relief, because it gave him an excuse to stay in Glen Dorcha a day and not continue his journey to Stiegle. Malcolm did not expect his runners to work miracles.

On the way back, he was asked the question he had been expecting: "Is it true the kelpie nearly got you?"

"Skin of my teeth. And a lot of other skin, too. Rorie arrived just in time."

More quietly: "Rorie of Ytter? That one? Is it true that he can perform miracles?"

"Well... wonders. But his wonders have a nasty whiplash—do *not* risk asking him for one! He'll give you whatever you ask for, but it will not be what you want."

"You've seen this?" Taran asked skeptically.

"Oh, yes, I've seen it. I tried to refuse his help last night in case I brought the curse down on me. But he helped me in spite of my pleas, so it didn't apply." He hoped. If he was wrong, he would soon find out.

By the time they returned, Rorie was sitting up and dressing, as were most of the hall's inhabitants. Ivor found his clothes, still damp in places and scorched in others, all spotted with blood. There were tears in his leggings and smock, but his shirt and cloak seemed to be whole, and he made himself respectable, except for the glimpses of hairy leg and bandages. By the time women began arriving to cook breakfast, he was sitting on the end of a bench to watch, aware that it was a long time since he'd dined on the king's meat pies. He enjoyed the familiar bustle. Truth be told, the private room in Stiegle was a welcome sign of his status as chief runner, but he did sometimes feel lonely there, missing the kennel-like crush of the runners' shed, and even the hall at Glenbroch before that.

Then suddenly Thane Elpin was looming over him. "You come with me, boy. You brought me a message, and I want to hear exactly what it says—in private."

Just as he had on his first visit to Dorcha, Ivor got a strong feeling that the thane didn't want anyone to know about his marriage plans. It seemed strange, although Malcolm had warned that such talk was always confidential because people could lose face if the negotiations failed.

"Aye, my lord." Ivor fumbled for the crutches lying at his feet and managed to stand up, steadied by Rorie's hand on his shoulder. It seemed Rorie expected to go with him.

"This is nothing to do with you, sellsword!" Elpin barked.

"With all due respect, my lord," Rorie said in an offensive drawl, "it is exactly my business. The king sent me after Ivor to see he got home safely."

Which was not what he'd told Ivor in the night.

"Are you hinting that he isn't safe in my hall?"

After an even more insulting pause, Rorie said, "No, my lord, although if I had caught up with him five minutes later last night, your nasty guard dog would have killed him. I am merely quoting my orders from the king." He raised a hand, which in Scone had been slathered in jewels and gold, but here bore a single silver ring, obviously a match for Ivor's, inscribed with the royal boar.

While Rorie's red-gold ponytail was not as blatant as the thane's ginger bush, they were definitely a pair of redheads facing off, and the hall had fallen into a shocked silence.

Ivor decided he had better intervene before these fire-eaters began tearing chunks off each other.

"Don't be ridiculous, Rorie! Of course I am safe in the thane's hall, and the message I brought is confidential."

For a moment he thought neither man was going to back down. Then Rorie said, "I'll come and wait outside the door."

"You'll wait outside the glen!" Elpin snapped. "I'll have no more of your insolence. Begone now, before I set the dogs on you."

"You won't. The runner and I are the king's men on the king's business. The runner is in no fit state to travel, and you are required to grant him food and shelter until he is."

"But not you. I don't have to feed any out-of-work sellsword who wanders in looking for charity."

Rorie said, "I stay where the boy stays, or would you have me ride back to Scone and tell Constantine that you prevented me from carrying out the duties he laid upon me?"

It was an absurd challenge, and completely unnecessary so far as Ivor could see. Elpin lowered his head and breathed hard like a provoked bull, then abruptly spun on his heel and headed for his room at the end. Ivor hobbled after him—and Rorie went along too.

"What was all that for?" Ivor demanded—quietly.

"Information. I'll explain when you're older."

"How much older?"

"Fifteen minutes, maybe."

"You!" Elpin said, hailing a greybeard who was kneeling at the end of the hall, rolling up his blanket. "You, Sawney. Watch that this freeloading snoop doesn't eavesdrop on my talk wi' this lad." He held the door for Ivor to limp through, and then shut it loudly. "Now the message!"

"Aye, my lord." Ivor straightened up as best he could on two poles and one foot. He opened his mouth and was struck with sudden panic, finding his mind a blank, as if the horrible events of the previous night had wiped it clean. The king had said... was it, *After further consideration...?* No, that was the one to Malcolm alone.

Then the fog lifted and he could begin. *"Constantine II, by the Grace of God, King of the Scots and Picts, Lord of Alba, sends greetings to our loyal and beloved Mormaor of the Isles, and to his stalwart servant, Thane Elpin of Glen Dorcha, saying: For us to approve the union you propose would cause a drastic change in the balance of power in our kingdom, and therefore we require that you justify it in person to our council when next it meets, here in Scone, on Candlemas Day. Thus spake the king."*

Elpin, predictably, was glowering. "That's not a 'No!'. You told me last night he said 'No!' but now you tell me that's not what he said."

Ivor was miserably aware that this was true; it wasn't a complete denial, although it was very close to one. Meg wasn't safe yet. "I was out on my feet last night, my lord. I'm sorry if I misled you."

"Useless trash. Get out.... But I'll have some words to send back to Malcolm when you leave."

"I'll need a horse, my lord. Mine got eaten by the kelpie."

Elpin rounded on him furiously. "And whose fault was that, when the loch's clearly marked with a warning? Didna' Dorsten tell you about it when you came in the first time? Now get out of my sight. And mind that you don't go gossiping about my business."

"My lord," Ivor said, struggling to hide his anger, "the mormaor's runners *never* discuss his business, even among themselves. I don't allow it."

After a struggle with the door, he did leave, finding Rorie outside, although not close to enough to eavesdrop. He was deep in conversation with old Sawney. Ignoring them, Ivor headed at speed to where porridge was being ladled out. It came with deliciously thick cream, too, and he had trouble keeping up with his neighbours' conversation, although little of it was to do with him or the kelpie—they seemed to prefer to ignore that monster. What interested them was Rorie of Ytter and his curse. Could he really work miracles?

Having witnessed St. Seumas work a genuine divine miracle not too long ago, Ivor would only confirm that Rorie had achieved some amazing favours for people, but they always did their recipients more harm than good.

After a while the mead hall settled down to the usual activities of a hird in winter, men engaged in sword practice and wrestling, women spinning, children squabbling noisily and racing around everywhere. Dogs kept coming to sniff the stranger suspiciously.

"Look after this for me," Rorie said, appearing at Ivor's side and dropping his belt knife on the table. All men carried a knife, but his was typically grander than most, with silver fretwork on the sheath and a huge cairngorm glowing like the moon on its pommel.

"Wait! I've aged quite a bit, so now you can tell me why you were riling the thane like that!"

Rorie grinned and leaned a forearm on the table, to bring his mouth down close to Ivor's ear. "I told you," he said softly. "For information. Didn't you see what happened?"

"Elpin got mad at you."

"Aye, but that was *all* that happened! I've been in more mead halls than there were fleas jumping around in here last night, and if I'd tried sassing the thane like that in any other one, there would have been six or eight of his youngest, largest housecarls closing in around me, flexing their shoulders and breathing on their knuckles. Now I gotta go and make some friends." He straightened up and strode away.

Ivor worked it out. It was true that nobody had come forward to relieve Elpin of his tormentor. Malcolm had told Ivor that the best way to judge a thane was to find out how his men felt about him. Rorie had just supplied the answer, but he had done it in a way that Ivor would never have dared attempt.

And soon he saw that Rorie had equally strange ideas about how to make friends. He had joined a gang of the younger housecarls preparing to practise their swordplay, but evidently he had scorned that idea. Ivor knew his opinion of sword fighting—that it was nine-tenths physical strength, shoving your shield against your opponent's and trying to push him off balance. Now he and one of the locals were stripping down to their britches, obviously about to try wrestling. The others spread out to form a ring; women and children climbed on benches to watch.

The two combatants circled each other warily. Then the local boy leaped forward to grapple, but something went wrong and he landed on his back with a crash. Yelling a furious obscenity he scrambled up and went to try again—with the same result. Was there anything that Rorie wasn't good at? Jeering friends hauled the boy away and another man came forward. And after the visitor dealt with him in much the same way, a third came to try, probably the largest man in the glen, shaggy-chested and about Rorie's age. He was more cautious with this deadly stranger.

Ivor did not have a good view from where he was sitting, but he had no desire to go and wobble on one foot anywhere close to that noisy crowd of spectators. Even one excited three-year-old might knock him flying. He had watched such scenes hundreds of times in Glenbroch, and would likely see them often again in Stiegle once winter closed in. From what he could make out, though, Dorcha standards were not up to Glenbroch's, and when Rorie conceded to his third opponent, he assumed that the visitor was being tactful. He had done enough to prove himself.

The wrestling was followed by a beer drinking session,

which was undoubtedly what Rorie had been after all along, with much laughter, back slapping, and shouts for the serfs to bring refills. By lunchtime he would have collected all the gossip available. It was clear now that Constantine had not sent Rorie along to babysit Ivor, or at least that had not been the main reason. The sellsword had been telling the truth when he said that he was supposed to investigate rumours of strange events in Glen Dorcha. What was the curse that had visited Elpin with so many deaths in the last two years? Why had no housecarls stepped forward to teach the impudent visitor a lesson? And why was the thane so frantically anxious not to let his hird know that he was trying to negotiate a second marriage?

Chapter 10

Although edible, Dorcha's bread was not as good as Stiegle's, but its superb cheese made up for it. As Ivor was finishing off a three-bap lunch, Rorie paused on the way past to collect his knife. He mentioned that the rain had stopped.

"We could start for home, then, maybe?"

"You canna' ride with that ankle, lad."

"Then I'll ride without it! I have a message to deliver."

"It will have to wait." Rorie strode away, leaving Ivor fuming, but helpless.

The hall gradually emptied as men and women went off to attend to outdoor work. Ivor remained, locked in frustration and winter boredom, and his mood was not helped when Rorie passed by again, this time with some of the local men, all talking about horses.

Not long after that, though, Taran, the young swordsman who had donated the crutches, came wandering over to him laden with horse gear, which he dumped on the table. He was followed by a serf, who brought a basket containing rags, brushes, and other necessary equipment, and then departed.

This was very obviously a hint that a visitor might as well pay for his keep by making himself useful, but the care of harnesses was normally serfs' work, so the young housecarl's real purpose must be something else. Was he just personally nosey, or had he been ordered to see what he could learn from the stranger?

"How's the ankle?" Taran asked as he sat down and selected a bridle to examine. He smiled the tolerant smile of a man whose chin could grow hair to a boy whose chin couldn't.

"It's a damnable nuisance, but it would be ten times worse without the crutches. Let me give you a hand."

Taran said that was a kind offer and handed him a collection of brass bits coated with dried spittle and crushed grass.

"Where did my minder go, do you know?" Ivor asked.

"Just that he rode off up the glen with Sawney. That's a fine roan he's got."

Ivor agreed that Hillrunner was exceptional. His turn: "What is there to see up the glen?"

"Kine, cows, and cattle." All of which were the same thing, of course. "How soon will you be able to ride, you suppose?"

"I think I could ride now, as long as my mount behaved itself. I'll make sure I leave here in daylight, though."

"Even in daylight," Taran said, "you'd better have company."

Thinking of the dark path under the trees, Ivor suppressed a shudder. "The kelpie hunts in daylight, too?"

"Sometimes. It's been known, but it only ever preys on folk who travel alone. Have you far to go?"

"Far enough. Drosten and I only just made it in daylight. I could run it easily enough in summer, but not in this weather."

That forced Taran to ask if he could really run faster than a horse could, which diverted the conversation away from the question of Ivor's destination. He was beginning to enjoy the game, and suspected that his companion was, too. But then the housecarl suddenly pinned him—or put him in check, depending on what they were playing.

"What's that buckle of yours mean?"

A pox on him! "It's a sign that I work for Mormaor Malcolm."

Taran's eyes twinkled with triumph. "And who gave you the fancy ring?"

Ivor held it up for him to see.

"A boar? But that's.... You work for the mormaor *and the king too?*"

"I'm Malcolm's captain of runners. The ring is a sign of royal approval, is all. It doesn't do much except when I visit Scone. It makes men jump through hoops there, though!"

"You've met the king?" Taran said, impressed.

I had lunch with him yesterday. "Aye. Fine gentleman, he is."

"You run messages for him too?"

No. I just win wars for him. Thane Elpin had guessed that Ivor was the hero who'd brought the Northmen to fight in the Battle of Nilcaster, and Drosten would certainly have been told about that during his stay in Stiegle, but the news had obviously not filtered down to the swordsmen of the hird. Why not? The Glen Dorcha men had been with

DAVE DUNCAN

Constantine's army, on the other side of the country, but Nilcaster had won the war for them, too.

"I do whatever he tells me!" Ivor said, making it a joke.

Taran didn't laugh. He had forgotten the tack cleaning and was staring hard at Ivor. "Your helper has a ring like it."

"Aye, he does."

"The king sent two men here to Dorcha?"

"Aye."

Taran looked all around uneasily, then lowered his voice. "Can I do anything to help?"

Checkmate! And a clear admission that something was far wrong in the glen. "Aye," Ivor said yet again. "Happens you could. I need to know if I can ride a horse with my ankle all trashed like this."

Taran pulled a face. "Man, I saw you stripped last night—you're one big bruise all over. You really want to try?"

"My business is urgent." It wasn't fair to keep Meg in suspense any longer than absolutely necessary.

"If you're sure you can...."

Ivor leaned down to get his crutches, wincing at the stab of pain in his ribs. "Let's go and see."

▶ ▼ ◀

The trouble, Taran joked as they left the hall, would be finding a horse tall enough and stirrup leathers long enough. Ivor was struggling too hard with crutches in mud to remember to laugh. It was a fine afternoon, although signs of fresh snow on the higher peaks showed that winter was coming, and the breeze was chill, swirling their cloaks around. When they reached the corral, where a dozen or so horses were gloomily waiting for hay time, there being no grass there to graze, Taran beckoned a serf.

"Alfred, our guest wants to go for a wee ride. Fetch Holy Terror for me, but he'll need something gentle."

"Springtime could use the exercise," the man said. From his name and accent, he was a Saxon, but he was too old to have been captured in this year's war. Springtime was a grey mare, clearly carrying a foal, but the ostler obviously thought that she could manage Ivor as well.

The problem was getting mounted without Rorie's strong arm to lift him and without crying out at the pain in his ribs. He managed it, but his left foot was so bundled in bandages that only his toes would fit in the stirrup; they were going to get very cold.

"All right?" Taran asked, looking up at him with concern—perhaps wondering what happened to anyone who injured a king's man.

"Fine," Ivor gasped. "Let's go."

The housecarl swung up into his saddle like a bird in flight. Holy Terror at once tried to send him winging off elsewhere, but failed, and after a few bucks and jumps accepted the inevitable and calmed down. Taran grinned triumphantly.

"Where to, Your Highness?"

"Up the glen." Ivor wanted to see what Rorie was doing, because he didn't trust Rorie to tell him about it later.

▶ ▼ ◀

The trail was a wide and reasonably level cart track, in much better condition than the path down to the loch. The reason for this became obvious very soon, when the riders passed a serf leading in an ox cart laden with peat.

"You sure about this?" Taran asked. "You're awful peaky looking."

"I'm fine!" Ivor said through clenched teeth. If the weather stayed good and he didn't show up in Stiegle within another two or three days, Malcolm would be sending the others out to look for him, and that would be humiliating. To turn the conversation away from himself, and because he couldn't think of any subtle way to ask about the thane's curse, he added, "How long has Elpin been thane?"

"A little more than half a year. Thane Breth died just before the king sent the fiery cross to call us to war."

That was not what Drosten had said!

"He couldn't have been tanist very long, then?"

Taran took so long to answer that Ivor thought he wasn't going to. Then it came in a rush: "Less than two weeks. His dad was tanist before him, Tanist Forcus. Forcus was well liked and not really old when he died, see, so we all thought it would be fair to elect his boy, Elpin, because he would have time to grow into the job—Thane Breth being young and strong, good for years yet, we thought. There weren't that many sons of Uven who were suitable.... But then Breth had his accident, so Elpin was thane."

That all sounded more like an apology than an explanation. Add in a dead wife and a bad smell became a real stench.

"What sort of accident?"

Taran nodded ahead. "At the bridge. I'll show you when we get there."

Now Ivor knew what Sawney and Rorie had gone to look at. "And that happened *before* the fiery cross came?"

Another long pause, as Taran squirmed between loyalty to his thane and loyalty to his king.... "Aye. But we'd heard rumours. We sort of knew it was coming."

"And how did Tanist Forcus die—Elpin's father?"

"Bad tooth. The blacksmith pulled it for him, but too late. It festered. His face swelled up like a haggis. Nasty way to die."

Yes, it was, but at least it didn't sound like murder. The

THE RUNNER AND THE KELPIE

tanist dies; his son is elected to take his place; the thane is going to lead the hird to war. The young tanist would not be the first man to have dreams of glory, nor the first to murder his lord. If Malcolm had known of this shadow over the man, would he have considered for a single moment marrying Meg to him? The king must have heard some of the story; that was why he had sent Rorie to investigate.

"And Elpin's wife? How did she die? And when?"

Taran turned an agonized face to Ivor. "Must I? I feel such a snitch!"

"You sound to me like an honourable man who's been badly betrayed," Ivor said. "Loyalty and honour should work both ways, you know. What I've been told is that her name was Lilias. Thunder wakened her one stormy night and she heard the horses upset, so she went out to calm them, got lost in the dark, and drowned in the loch."

"And you *believe* it?" Taran shouted. "She was still nursing her baby, so she might have been sleeping lightly. But to go out on a night like that when she first had to walk through a hall full of serfs and freemen snoring their heads off? She'd have given one of them a hard kick in the ass and sent him out instead, wouldn't she?"

Of course she would. And it was good half mile to the loch—why would she ever walk that far through a thunderstorm? "When did this happen?"

"Less than a month ago."

"Oh, Saints!" Ivor whispered. Had that been the same night he'd had the nightmare? Drosten had told Meg it happened a year ago. No wonder the thane was trying to keep his marriage hopes secret! The man was a monster, but how could anyone prove it?

In the subsequent silence, Ivor became aware again of pulses of pain in his ribs that seemed to syncopate with those from his ankle. He also realized that the trail was climbing a sort of ramp up a long ridge that wound across the glen. A man was standing on the skyline beside two horses. Soon Ivor recognized him as old Sawney, but even when he reached the crest, he could see no sign of Rorie. *Where was he? Had there been another "accident"?*

Beyond the ridge, the glen was one wall-to-wall peat bog. In the distance serfs were cutting and stacking peats to dry for next year and another cart was being loaded to provide heat in the hall over the coming winter. It was a familiar Alban scene.

Where Sawney was holding the horses, the road crossed a narrow gash, the bed of a mountain stream cutting through the ridge. The little canyon was maybe twenty feet deep. Rorie must have climbed down to investigate, because now he was scrambling up the steep gravelly wall. The bridge was made of tree trunks and was barely wide enough for an oxcart. It would be narrow for two men riding abreast.

"This is where Thane Breth died?"

Taran nodded miserably. "It gets icy sometimes. The fog had come in. They were heading home, and the thane went in front. Elpin heard him cry out...."

"Just the two of them, thane and tanist?" No other witnesses?

"Just the two of them."

A wagon or cart would be fairly stable during the crossing, because its wheels would fit in the dips between the logs. But two men together would normally ride side by side, and the footing would not be as safe for horses. If one rider suddenly spurred his horse so it stumbled into the other one on a slippery and uneven surface like that, then horse and rider might easily plunge over the edge and drop onto boulders.

There were other ways it might have been arranged, but that would have been the simplest, and even explicable if it failed, for it could all be blamed on a clumsy horse.

But you could never prove it.

Chapter 11

Rorie straightened up, slapping dirt off his hands. Scowling at Ivor, he retrieved Hillrunner's reins from the greybeard Sawney, and came over to him.

"You are a pigheaded young idiot. You should be resting, not trying to make your injuries worse. Let's go." He swung up into the saddle.

Ivor hurt too much to argue. He turned Springtime and the two of them rode slowly back down the slope. He glanced back to make sure Sawney and Taran were not within earshot.

"So what do you think happened back there?" he asked.

Rorie pulled a face. "God and his angels know. What the thane told everyone at the time was that he and Breth were on their way home when fog closed in. Breth was in a hurry and went on in front. If you believe that much, it sounds like they'd quarrelled. Elpin says he heard a cry, and when he got to the bridge he could hear groans, so he hobbled his horse and climbed down. He found Breth unconscious and pinned under his horse, which was dead. Since he couldn't move it by himself, he climbed back up, rode to the hall, and returned with help, but by then Breth was dead too."

"And do you believe that?"

"No. Do you?"

"I wish there had been other witnesses," Ivor said.

"That means no. I can believe they quarrelled. Why d'you suppose the thane took his new young tanist up the glen in the first place? They'd heard that there was going to be a war summons, so likely Breth had already begun calling in his men from outlying areas. But he couldn't take them all. You have to leave someone to watch your serfs, or they'll vanish over the skyline as soon as your back's turned, right?"

"Right."

"Most of Dorcha's serfs work in the peat cutting, and it's possible that the two freemen went up to look over the situation, and Breth might—only might, because I'm guessing—have told Elpin that he was going to be left in charge of the glen while the thane was gone. No war for him. And that would have started young Elpin wondering if he would be too old to lead the hird by the time the next war came along. This could be his only chance."

Ivor's suspicions hadn't gone that far, but it all made sense. He nodded. Thinking about murder helped keep his mind off his ankle, which was burning like a smith's forge.

"Still guessing," Rorie said grimly, "quarrel or not, I think they were riding side by side when they reached the slippery bridge. They may have both been tight-lipped about something, but not to have ridden together would have been a childish display of temper. Elpin may have been planning it, or it may have been an impulse, but I suspect he either rammed his horse into Breth's or stuck his knife in it to make it shy; over they went. Then he climbed down and made sure that his victim was safely dead. I was looking for boulders with bloodstains on them just now, but I didn't find any. What do you think?"

"I agree. But how do you prove it?"

"You can't. Not ever. The housecarls must have been suspicious, dammit! They'd have checked, questioned, looked.... They're not stupid, but they had to give Elpin the benefit of the doubt. So they gave him three cheers as their new thane and elected Eddarrnonn as replacement tanist. Looks like we're going to have company."

Three riders were approaching from the hall, still too distant to identify, but Ivor thought he could guess who one of them would be.

"The thane doesn't like us prying."

"Wouldn't bet against that," Rorie said. "Your turn now—tell me what you think happened to Lady Lilias last month."

"My turn to guess, you mean. Maybe he was just tired of her. She'd given him a second daughter and some men only want sons. Maybe he got off so easily with one murder that another felt like a good idea."

It was also possible, Ivor realized now, that Elpin might have felt the hird's distrust of him growing and thought he would be safer if he was married to Earl Malcolm's daughter, for the mormaor would stand up for his son-in-law. Of course Ivor couldn't mention the marriage proposal to Rorie. And the king's response made more sense now. Even the king could not depose a thane without good reason—the man's hird would leap to his defence, because that was their duty and purpose. But if the king could get Elpin before his Great Council, then he might denounce him there, and the Council could take some action, perhaps.

Repeating what Taran had said, Ivor added, "Elpin's story doesn't make much sense because to go outside and calm the horses, she'd have had to walk the length of the hall, where the serfs sleep. If she was too scared of her husband to waken him and tell him he had a problem, she could have sent a serf to do the job."

"Nobody saw her leave the hall," Rorie said. "It was a noisy night, so you'd think someone would have been awake. And her maids testified that she definitely had gone to bed—in her husband's bed."

"I think he murdered her," Ivor agreed. "I can't believe he tied her up and gagged her and carried her out over his shoulder without being seen, but I think he arranged it somehow. Again, no one can ever prove it!"

"Here comes the suspect," Rorie said. "Start smiling. We don't want him to know we're talking about him."

The man in the centre was Thane Elpin. Flanking him were Tanist Eddarrnonn and his trusty, Drosten of Cleish. The tanist puzzled Ivor. He seemed to be quite loyal to Elpin, ignoring any scandal or rumours, but if the housecarls had been suspicious of Forcus's death, you would have expected them to elect a tanist who thought that way too.

The threesome halted, blocking the road. Their expressions were grim. Obviously it was eviction time. Ivor and Rorie reined in. In a moment Taran reined in next to Rorie, and Sawney beside Ivor. Silence.

"Did the king order you to spy on us?" Elpin barked suddenly. He was making no effort to hide his anger.

Rorie said, "No, my lord." He was a good liar.

"Then why are you doing it?"

"We're not. I rode up there because my horse needs some exercise every day. The boy came later because he was young enough to think he's indestructible. He's a little older and wiser now."

Elpin sneered in disbelief. "Did the king not tell you to work some miracles for us? Both of you have the reputation of working miracles."

Rorie looked to Ivor in pretend surprise. "Did he ask you that?"

"No, Freeman. He gave me a message to deliver to both the thane, which I did, and the mormaor, which I haven't been able to do yet."

Rorie turned back to Elpin, smiling mockingly. "And I try my best never to perform miracles. My miracles always have unfortunate side effects."

"Well you'll do none here." The thane glanced up at the sky. The sun was very close to the top of the western hills. "The boy can stay on a day or two, till his foot heals, but you go now. You've just got time to pass the loch before dark. You can sleep in the shelter at the far end."

Rorie opened his mouth, but whatever he was about to say was cut off by a shout from old Sawney. "No! Freeman Rorie of Ytter, I beg you to—"

"Stop!" Rorie was even louder. "You must not ask me for any favours!"

"Shut up, Sawney!" Thane Elpin added.

"I will not shut up!" the old man yelled. *"I must know what happened to my daughter. Freeman Rorie, I beg you to find that out for me!"*

His daughter? Ivor realized with horror that Sawney must mean Lilias.

"Oh, Hel's claws!" Rorie groaned.

By the terms of his curse he could not refuse the appeal, and no matter how impossible the task, he would succeed, but then Sawney—if he even survived—would wish he had never asked. Elpin seemed to know the rules, too, for his face above the red beard had turned pale; whether from rage or fear Ivor could not tell.

"Well you'll have to hurry, Rorie of Ytter," the thane said.

"The sun is about to set and you have to pass the loch. Let's see this miracle."

Rorie said nothing. He fumbled in his purse, and when his fingers found what he wanted, he reached across Ivor to hand something tiny to the old man.

Sawney took it and cried out in horror. "Her wedding ring! I'd know it anywhere. Three garnets it had. One of them's gone, but the other two.... Look at it—Eddarrnonn, Drosten, you know it don't you?"

Drosten took it, looked at it, and then passed it to Elpin, who leaned away from it as if it might bite him. The mood had changed already, as if the sun had suddenly vanished. Now both Eddarrnonn and Drosten had turned their frowns on Elpin.

"Where did you get that, Freeman?" Sawney demanded.

"Aye!" said the tanist. "Where?"

"I won't tell you," Rorie said. "But I'll take you there and show you."

Chapter 12

They rode in silence back to the hall, Elpin in the lead, Rorie and Ivor next, and the others following. When they reached it, Rorie told Ivor, "You stay here," and the thane, "We're going to need torches and a tinderbox." Elpin shouted orders to a serf, who ran to fetch what was needed.

Ivor said, "Not for all the gold in Rome." He knew now where Rorie was going, but not what he expected to find there.

No one else said anything, and in a few minutes the same seven riders continued on toward the loch, watched in puzzled silence by serfs, housecarls, women, and even children. They all seemed to sense the dread mood.

Ivor's skin puckered up in goose bumps when the shadows of the trees closed over him, and Springtime flicked her ears as she sensed his fear, but she kept on, following Hillrunner. It had been about halfway along the loch that Rorie had marked the tree, Ivor thought—right beside one of the water gaps, where the kelpie could come ashore. He was caught by surprise when Rorie halted.

"About here, my lord." Rorie dismounted and handed his reins up to Ivor to hold. Elpin rode past them—which was a tight squeeze—to watch from the far side. Ivor stayed mounted; the rest crowded in on foot, leaving Taran at the rear holding their horses. It wasn't quite dark, but the light was very poor. Someone struck flint and in a moment their torches were flaming and illuminated the scene.

"Right here," Rorie said. "When the boy and I were coming in last night, I saw something glitter. So I got down and took a look. That's where I found the ring, down there in the muck. No one would have seen anything unless they happened to come by in the dark with a light, as I did, and I wouldn't have done that if young Ivor had understood the kelpie warning. I marked the tree, but you can see that my cut's not the only mark. Lower down, it looks as if the bark's been scored by ropes, see?"

Sawney pushed his way to the front and dropped to his knees. Eddarrnonn held a torch closer.

"Aye!" the tanist said. "There's even a few fibres caught in the bark."

"Now look in the dirt," Rorie suggested. His voice was grim.

Sawney did so, scratching it up and letting it filter through his fingers. He found something.... He shrieked in horror.

Rorie's curse had claimed another victim.

"What's he found?" Taran demanded from the back of the group.

He had found Ivor's nightmare.

"Bones," Rorie said. "Little bones, picked clean. Finger bones from a woman's hands. Her killer must have gagged her and tied her up. He slid her out through the window and probably put her over a horse's back to bring her down to the loch. He laid her down there, by the water gap, and tied her bonds to that tree to make sure she stayed there. And then, I'm sure, he leaped on his horse and rode like a madman back out of the forest."

"And the kelpie...?"

Rorie had to raise his voice over Sawney's wails. "The kelpie came and dragged her into the loch, but her hands wouldn't pass through the bonds, so they were torn apart. And in the morning someone—I won't say who—came and took away any rope that remained. He probably kicked some of the mulch over any other evidence, counting on field mice to remove it."

There was wild splashing as a horse clattered through the water gap, then thumping as it sped away along the path. With shouts of, "Stop him!" men tried to reach their horses, but Ivor turned Springtime and Hillrunner to block them, and Rorie shouted, "Let him go! If God has any justice in this world...."

Silence fell. They listened. Minutes dragged by until Ivor was certain the fleeing thane must have cleared the lake and so escaped the kelpie. But then something screamed horribly in the far distance. Whether it was Elpin, or his horse, or the kelpie itself, Ivor could not tell—and did not want to know. But, yes, there was justice.

Eddarrnonn began to murmur an Ave for the dead man's soul, and the others joined in, some more willingly than others. The one exception was old Sawney, who was sobbing uncontrollably. His wish had been granted. Now, knowing the horrible fate that had been meted out to his daughter, he was so shattered by grief that he was incapable of doing anything, even mounting his horse. Taran and Eddarrnonn took turns walking him home along the narrow path, while their horses were led.

He wasn't the only one who'd had too much of that day. When they reached the hall, Rorie lifted Ivor out of the saddle and carried him inside, quieting his protests by telling him he didn't weigh any more than a good fat haggis. Eddarrnonn said to put him on the thane's bed, because he was going home to his wife and didn't need it yet.

▶ ▼ ◀

Next day it rained, so nobody was going anywhere, although a search of the low road did turn up Elpin's sword and his horse, dead of a broken neck. Of the man himself there was no sign. The housecarls cheered Eddarrnonn as their thane, and plans were made for a meeting to elect a new tanist. Ivor was told to stay where he was, and so he lay on his back all day, wondering how long it would take him to save up enough money to own a feather mattress like that one.

When the sun came out, the day after, big Bula brought a shoe to replace the one he had lost. The swelling had gone down a lot, so he found he was able to hobble around on a cane. He insisted he must leave, and Rorie wryly agreed to see him safely home to Stiegle, since he obviously wasn't capable of looking after himself. The new thane presented him with a complete set of clothes, specially sewed for him, and also gave him Springtime as a non-wedding gift to Lady Meg. Ivor rode out of Glen Dorcha in style, with no regrets, and no plans ever to return.

▶ ▼ ◀

They took it easy, for the streams were all bank-full again, but Ivor was very glad to stop whenever his companion suggested it. It was amazing how many friends Rorie had—scattered around all over Alba, it seemed—who were willing to put him up for the night. Ivor slept in the haylofts. Not long after noon on the third day, they came within sight of Stiegle.

"Here I leave you," Rorie said. He preferred to keep his distance from Malcolm, who had once sentenced him to be hanged. "I must go and report to our friend in Scone, although I imagine he's heard from Eddarrnonn by now."

"Thank you, Freeman. I don't know what I'd have done without you."

Rorie laughed. "I do, and it isn't pleasant. God go with you, young Ivor, and may he continue to give you good luck in your new career."

"What new career?"

The sellsword shrugged. "Just a hunch I've got. You're wasted as a runner, lad."

"Runners do important work!"

"So they do. Some other men do more important work, though. God bless!"

He didn't specify which god he meant. You could never tell with Rorie.

Chapter 13

It was nice to come home. As Ivor started up the hill to the fort, letting Springtime choose her own pace and looking forward to seeing the expression of relief on Meg's face when he told her his news, he met Galan and Ilgarach on their way out for a run.

"What happened to you?" Galan demanded. Obviously Ivor's bruises had not yet faded into invisibility, as he had hoped.

"More important—what happened to Gawkie?" asked Ilgarach.

"We had an accident," Ivor said, for he could never keep that part of his story secret. "I sprained an ankle. Gawkie got eaten. No, sorry, I have to report to Malcolm first. Maybe tell you tomorrow?"

Chuckling at their angry protests, he rode on. He saw the faint trail leading off to Gruoch's hovel, and made a mental note to take her another gift so he could tell her how her prophecy had worked out. When he reached the gate, the guards there cheered his approach. The man in charge was his old friend Eoghan.

"What did you do to the other guy, Runner?"

"Oh, it was nothing. There were only three of them." This time he was jeered as he rode away. They didn't believe him!

He got some odd looks on his ride to the stable, but did not stop to be questioned. The next person he spoke to was Sean, the ancient hostler. His eyesight was probably too bad to notice Ivor's face, but he knew that a gravid mare wasn't gelding Gawkie. More explanations were needed.

"We had an accident, and Gawkie died. This is Springtime, a gift to Lady Meg. Send my bag to the armoury, will you, please? Is the mormaor home, do you know?" If his horse was, then he was.

Sean shook his head, which looked like a tortoise's: hairless, toothless, and perched on a scraggy neck. "Nay, Runner, he went hunting three days ago. Expect him home soon."

Cursing quietly, Ivor dismounted, stretched to ease the knots out, then took his cane, and limped off in the direction of the armoury. Before he had gone far, he decided that there was no reason he couldn't tell Meg that Elpin was dead. That wasn't a secret! He changed direction. The guards on the door reported his arrival and were told to admit him.

Meg and Lady Kenina had been weaving, but they hurried over to the door to greet him, and exclaimed in dismay at his bruises and his limp. He bowed to each in turn; they asked what had happened to him.... Then the two servant girls were sent away, with orders to fetch mead, and Ivor was seated between the ladies in front of the fire. It was a nice welcome, and he tried hard to be attentive to Lady Kenina and not just smile witlessly at Meg all the time.

"So, Runner, what news have you brought us?"

"You know where I went," he said, for Meg had been present when he received his orders. "I return with shocking news, for Thane Elpin will not be marrying anyone. He has been called to judgment."

The ladies crossed themselves. Kenina probably said a prayer for the dead man's soul, but the length of time Meg sat with her eyes closed, her hands clasped, and a blissful expression on her face, suggested that she was saying a profound prayer of thanks. Her mother frowned in disapproval. Then the girl with the mead arrived. Before she had even filled the goblets, in strode the mormaor himself, who demanded to know what had happened to Ivor, so he had to go back to the beginning again.

▶▼◀

For the next hour, Ivor sat beside the fire with the earl and the ladies, sipping mead, just as if he were one of the family. It was a heady experience. He could have reached out and taken Meg's hand, but he would have had to drink a whole flagon of mead to do anything as foolhardy as that. He told the whole story, repeating the king's messages, and then his narrow escape from the kelpie, which made the ladies cry out in horror, then Rorie, the uncovering of the thane's crimes, and even Springtime and her unborn foal.

When the time came to report the king's words, he was told to so without getting out the chair. The speech about the proposed marriage didn't apply anymore, of course, but it made Malcolm smile and nod, as if he had expected something like that. The other one, about Bishop Pol, made no more sense to Ivor than it had before. Again Malcolm nodded, but did not comment.

Meg rose and lit some candles, for night was falling, but Ivor suspected she was again giving thanks for her release.

"Very well done!" Malcolm said when the tale was done. "I think it's my turn to talk for a while."

"It certainly is!" his wife commented cryptically.

"Ivor of Glenbroch, I owe you an apology."

"Me, my lord?"

"You. I warned you it was complicated, lad. I am mormaor of the west, earl of Stiegle, and thane of several other places. Not all of my estates follow the same rules. These lands used to be part of Dalriada, before it joined with Pictland to make Alba. So whose laws and customs apply?"

Ivor knew only that he had no idea. Fortunately it was none of his business, and he wondered why the mormaor was bothering to tell him about it. He wanted to go off to the hall and eat, and then disappear into his closet and sleep. He was aware that Meg kept gazing at him, but he was the hero of the hour, so that was forgivable, but he mustn't stare at her. He really wanted to hug her so she could give him a big kiss as a reward for saving her from the horrible villain, Elpin. They all seemed to think that it had been all his doing, and he was starting to believe that himself.

Malcolm was still droning on. "Most thanes are elected by the housecarls—elected tanist, that is, to succeed the thane when he dies or retires. But my father seized a couple of thanedoms by force and appointed himself thane and me tanist to succeed him, which I did. The thanedom of Ardenfort belonged to Lady Kenina's father, and she brought it to me as her dowry.

"As if that isn't complicated enough, my wife gave me two sons and a daughter, but both our sons died as infants. We will have no more children now. When I die, Meg's husband, whoever he may be, will claim to be my heir. There is ample room for civil war in this problem."

Ivor gulped and glanced again at Meg, but she seemed to have lost interest in him and was staring at her mother. It must be embarrassing to have to listen to her father discussing her like a horse for sale, and before a minor servant like him.

"I discussed this with the king when I last saw him, at Christmastide, two years ago. He insisted that Meg must not marry some foreign prince who might meddle in this kingdom and still be loyal to some other ruler. I had to find her a loyal young Alban, whom I should train to succeed me. Thane Tasgall of Glenbroch seemed ideal, a highly respected swordsman familiar with this area. And Meg was willing."

"She never said she loved him!" Lady Kenina said quietly. "She said she would do her duty and if her duty was to marry that—I think 'giant' was the word she used—then she would do her best to be a good wife to him."

"Which is only proper," her father said reprovingly, implying that women should not interrupt men's talk without permission. "But he died in the war, so we had to start over. Promising young men are hard to find! By the time you find them, they have usually already promised themselves to a wife.

"As it happened, the king had sent me a suggestion as to who that young man might be. Constantine is a skilful judge of men, and he gave the lad in question a token of his approval, something he does not hand out lightly. I had never even given that youngster a thought, although I knew he was of good family and well mannered. I decided I would have to test him."

Why was Lady Kenina smiling like that? Why had Meg turned pale?

"Before I had time to think about it, I had to ride out to war, but suddenly I discovered a serious crisis brewing at my back. All the men I would normally send to deal with such a situation had gone south already. In desperation, I sent the youth I mentioned to try to handle it. I feared I was sending him to his death. It turned out that I wasn't, because he not only saved the Northman situation, he won the war for me. He became an instant hero throughout all Alba. No further tests were needed. He had proved his worth without a scrap of doubt."

Ivor gulped on a mouthful of mead, choked, and went into a coughing fit.

"When the war ended and we all got home again," Malcolm continued as if he hadn't noticed, "I sent Bishop Pol to confer with the king and his advisors. They all agreed it would be a good match and in view of your proven abilities, your present lack of rank would not be a problem. The lawyers suggested two ways I could proceed. I could marry you to my daughter and make you my son-in-law, or I could just adopt you as my son. Obviously we can't do both, because my son cannot marry my daughter.

"I can't order you to accept either. If you'd rather go back to Genbroch and become a housecarl in your brother's hird, we shall quite understand. If you'd prefer to be heir designate, then it's up to you whether you would rather do it by adoption or by marriage to my daughter."

"When he asked my opinion," Lady Kenina said, "I entirely agreed, but I suggested we wait a little while before proceeding, since the persons in question were moving in the right direction all by themselves."

Ivor looked to Meg and made an incoherent noise, which her mother ignored.

"For high-born ladies, the road to marriage is usually duty. A marriage without love is a torment, but fortunately love usually follows the wedding. When love comes first, that makes a much easier path, and it was obvious that Meg had found a, um, better giant."

Bleary-eyed from coughing, Ivor looked again at Meg and then at her mother. He gasped, "You knew?"

"Of course we knew, dear. The whole fort knows. When you went out running, she would call for her horse, and her guards would ride along behind, watching the two of you gazing into each other's eyes all the time. It was a wonder you didn't both trip and break your necks. And every time you thought nobody was looking, you wound up together like ivy on trees."

Arrrrgh! Was he as pink as Meg was now?

Malcolm laughed. "Considering what we had in mind, it really was quite funny to watch. But I swear I was on the point of calling you in to ask you sternly if your intentions toward my daughter were honourable, when along came the offer from Thane Elpin—youngish, fought well in the war, master of widespread lands adjoining mine. The hird he led to the war was one of the largest in the king's army. His wife had died a year ago, so we were told. Ignoring fairy tale notions of romance and love, he did seem like a good match.

"Moreover, a powerful thane like Elpin would not be pleased if I turned him down in favour of a penniless youth, one of my own servants, no matter how well his family was thought of. I warned you that marriage negotiations can lead to feuds and bloodshed.

"Furthermore, suppose Meg did marry Elpin, a very ambitious neighbour with hundreds of housecarls at his back? I didn't know of his murders, of course, but I did wonder if I might meet with an unfortunate hunting accident so he could succeed me. Heirs can be dangerous."

Ivor gulped and nodded.

"I sent you back with Drosten, not as a possible rival suitor but as my most trusted runner. Your message, Ivor, was intended to buy time, neither agreeing nor refusing, and I sent you on to the king. In effect, I was asking him to choose between the pair of you! He has that right, as my liege lord. Why are you grinning?"

Ivor hadn't been aware that he was grinning. "His Grace greeted me very, um, graciously, my lord. He must have thought you had sent me to tell him that... that..." *That Ivor of Glenbroch was to marry the earl's daughter?* It was too bizarre to put into words. And after that interview, the king had called in Rorie of Ytter and told him! Rorie had known all the time. And the two reasons he had given for following after Ivor had both been true—the king had told him to investigate the rumours he had heard about Glen Dorcha, but also to keep an eye on Ivor's safety.

Malcolm said, "Well, he obviously thought you were the better choice, because his reply to Thane Elpin was a tactfully phrased refusal. And now you bring the welcome news that the villain has met with justice!"

"So the next move is up to you, Ivor," Lady Kenina said.

Next what? He looked at the mormaor's expectant smile, then at the lady, and then at Meg—who nodded vigorously.

He rose unsteadily, leaning on the cane in case he fell over, which was not unlikely. He bowed to Malcolm.

He said, "My lord.... Um.... My lord, I, um...."

"'Humbly ask,'" Meg prompted, rising to stand beside him.

"Humbly ask, if..."

"'For!'" she said. "'For the hand of your daughter Meg...'"

"For the hand of your... really?" He was really doing this? Son-in-law to an earl, heir to one of the largest earldoms in Alba? *He? Little Ivor, the Runt?*

"Mm," Malcolm said thoughtfully. "Glenbroch? Are you by any chance related to Thane Angus?"

"Oh, stop tormenting him," his wife said. "We are very happy to agree, Ivor. You're too young for marriage yet, but you can certainly be betrothed, and if you both feel the same way in a year or so.... She's standing on tiptoe already, for heaven's sake! Go ahead and kiss her!"

"Wait!" Malcolm said. "You're not of age yet, so I shall have to send a runner to Glenbroch to get permission from the head of your family. That will be Thane Angus, I presume?"

"I'll be happy to attend to that errand personally, my lord," Ivor said. "Now excuse me—" He kissed his bride-to-be.

About the Author

Originally from Scotland, Dave Duncan has lived all his adult life in Western Canada, having enjoyed a long career as a petroleum geologist before taking up writing. Since discovering that imaginary worlds are more satisfying than the real one, he has published more than forty-five novels, mostly in the fantasy genre, but also young adult, science fiction, and historical. He has at times been Sarah B. Franklin (but only for literary purposes) and Ken Hood (which is short for "D'ye Ken Whodunit?")

His most successful works have been fantasy series: The Seventh Sword, A Man of His Word and its sequel, A Handful of Men, and six books about The King's Blades.

He and Janet were married in 1959. They have one son and two daughters, who in turn are responsible for a spinoff series of four grandchildren. Dave now lives in Victoria, BC.

Books by Five Rivers

NON-FICTION

Al Capone: Chicago's King of Crime, by Nate Hendley

Crystal Death: North America's Most Dangerous Drug, by Nate Hendley

Dutch Schultz: Brazen Beer Baron of New York, by Nate Hendley

Motivate to Create: a guide for writers, by Nate Hendley

Shakespeare for Slackers: Romeo and Juliet, by Aaron Kite, Audrey Evans and Jade Brooke

The Organic Home Gardener, by Patrick Lima and John Scanlan

Elephant's Breath & London Smoke: historic colour names, definitions & uses, Deb Salisbury, editor

Stonehouse Cooks, by Lorina Stephens

John Lennon: Music, Myth and Madness, by Nate Hendley

Shakespeare for Readers' Theatre: Hamlet, Romeo & Juliet, Midsummer Night's Dream, by John Poulson

Stephen Truscott, Decades of Injustice by Nate Hendley

FICTION

Black Wine, by Candas Jane Dorsey

88, by M.E. Fletcher

Immunity to Strange Tales, by Susan J. Forest

The Legend of Sarah, by Leslie Gadallah

Growing Up Bronx, by H.A. Hargreaves

North by 2000+, a collection of short, speculative fiction, by H.A. Hargreaves

A Subtle Thing, Alicia Hendley

Downshift, a Sid Rafferty Thriller, by Matt Hughes

Old Growth, a Sid Rafferty Thriller by Matt Hughes

Kingmaker's Sword, Book 1: Rune Blades of Celi, by Ann Marston

Western King, Book 2: The Rune Blades of Celi, by Ann Marston

Broken Blade, Book 3: The Rune Blades of Celi, by Ann Marston

Cloudbearer's Shadow, Book 4: The Rune Blades of Celi, by Ann Marston

King of Shadows, Book 5: The Rune Blades of Celi, by Ann Marston

Indigo Time, by Sally McBride

Wasps at the Speed of Sound, by Derryl Murphy

A Method to Madness: A Guide to the Super Evil, edited by Michell Plested and Jeffery A. Hite

A Quiet Place, by J.W. Schnarr

Things Falling Apart, by J.W. Schnarr

And the Angels Sang: a collection of short speculative fiction, by Lorina Stephens

From Mountains of Ice, by Lorina Stephens

Memories, Mother and a Christmas Addiction, by Lorina Stephens

Shadow Song, by Lorina Stephens

YA FICTION

My Life as a Troll, by Susan Bohnet

The Runner and the Wizard, by Dave Duncan

The Runner and the Saint, by Dave Duncan

The Runner and the Kelpie, by Dave Duncan

A Touch of Poison, by Aaron Kite

Out of Time, by D.G. Laderoute

Mik Murdoch: Boy-Superhero, by Michell Plested

Mik Murdoch: The Power Within, by Michell Plested

Type, by Alicia Hendley

FICTION COMING SOON

Cat's Pawn, by Leslie Gadallah

Cat's Gambit, by Leslie Gadallah

Sword and Shadow, Book 6: The Rune Blades of Celi, by Ann Marston

Bane's Choice, Book 7: The Rune Blades of Celi, by Ann Marston

A Still and Bitter Grave, by Ann Marston

Diamonds in Black Sand, by Ann Marston

NON-FICTION COMING SOON

Annotated Henry Butte's Dry Dinner, by Michelle Enzinas

King Kwong, by Paula Johanson

Shakespeare for Slackers: Hamlet, by Aaron Kite and Audrey Evans

Shakespeare for Slackers: Macbeth, by Aaron Kite and Audrey Evans

Shakespeare for Reader's Theatre, Book 2: Shakespeare's Greatest Villains, The Merry Wives of Windsor; Othello, the Moor of Venice; Richard III; King Lear, by John Poulsen

YA NON-FICTION COMING SOON

The Prime Ministers of Canada Series:
- Sir John A. Macdonald
- Alexander Mackenzie
- Sir John Abbott
- Sir John Thompson
- Sir Mackenzie Bowell
- Sir Charles Tupper
- Sir Wilfred Laurier
- Sir Robert Borden
- Arthur Meighen
- William Lyon Mackenzie King
- R. B. Bennett
- Louis St. Laurent
- John Diefenbaker
- Lester B. Pearson
- Pierre Trudeau
- Joe Clark
- John Turner
- Brian Mulroney
- Kim Campbell
- Jean Chretien
- Paul Martin

www.fiveriverspublishing.com

The Runner and the Wizard

by Dave Duncan

ISBN 9781927400395 $11.99

eISBN 9781927400401 $4.99

Trade Paperback 6 x 9, 100 pages

October 1, 2013

Young Ivor dreams of being a swordsman like his nine older brothers, but until he can grow a beard he's limited to being a runner, carrying messages for their lord, Thane Carrak. That's usually boring, but this time Carrak has sent him on a long journey to summon the mysterious Rorie of Ytter. Rorie is reputed to be a wizard—or an outlaw, or maybe a saint—but the truth is far stranger, and Ivor suddenly finds himself caught up in a twisted magical intrigue that threatens Thane Carrak and could leave Ivor himself very dead.

The Runner and the Saint

by Dave Duncan

ISBN 9781927400531 $11.99

eISBN 9781927400548 $4.99

Trade Paperback 6 x 9, 114 pages

March 1, 2014

Earl Malcolm has reason to fear the ferocious Northmen raiders of the Western Isles are going to attack the land of Alba, so he sends Ivor on a desperate mission with a chest of silver to buy them off. But the situation Ivor finds when he reaches the Wolf's Lair is even worse than he was led to expect. Only a miracle can save him now.

A Touch of Poison

by Aaron Kite

ISBN 9781927400593 $19.99

eISBN 9781927400609 $4.99

Trade Paperback 6 x 9, 234 pages

August 1, 2014

A 2012 Best Fantasy Watty Winner

Gwenwyn is the most miserable princess ever, and for good reason. Merely brushing up against her or touching her exposed skin is enough to cause painful burns, or worse. And if that wasn't enough, she's just discovered the singular reason for her existence — to act as the king's secret assassin, murdering neighboring princes with nothing more than a simple kiss.

The Legend of Sarah

by Leslie Gadallah

ISBN 9781927400517 $23.99

eISBN 9781927400524 $4.99

Trade Paperback 6 x 9, 234 pages

March 1, 2014

For Sarah, the one bright spot in her day is the storyteller's tales of the Old People, of their magically easy lives. And as darkness falls, if one of the wealthier listeners should happen to be so intent on the storyteller's voice as to become careless of his own purse, well so much the better. Inspired by the storyteller's narratives, Sarah often conceives of her own life as the stuff of legend for some future troubadour.

Only, such daydreams could never have prepared her for becoming embroiled with a witchy Phile, an agent of the devil come seeking the Old People's places. How could Sarah have known picking the wrong pocket could strand her in the middle of a power-struggle between Brother Parker, the Governor, and the encroaching Phile spies?

Type

by Alicia Hendley

ISBN 9781927400296 $31.99

eISBN 9781927400302 $9.99

Trade Paperback 6 x 9, 314 pages

June 1, 2013

After the fallout from the Social Media Era, when rates of divorce, crime, and mental illness were sky-rocketing, civilization was at its breaking point. As a result, prominent psychologists from around the globe gathered together to try to regain social order through scientific means.

Their solution? Widespread implementation of Myers-Briggs personality typing, with each citizen assessed at the age of twelve and then sent to one of sixteen Home Schools in order to receive the appropriate education for their Type and aided in choosing a suitable occupation and life partner.

North American society becomes structured around the tenets of Typology, with governments replaced by The Association of Psychologists. With social order seemingly regained, what could go possibly wrong?